BEFORE the GIANT ANTEATER

Peter Clarke

stories

Copyright © 2024 Peter Clarke

All rights reserved. No part of this publication may be reproduced, stored, or transmitted in any form or by any means, electronic, mechanical, photocopying, recording, scanning, or otherwise without written permission from the publisher. It is illegal to copy this book, post it to a website, or distribute it by any other means without permission.

The stories and characters are fictitious. Certain long-standing institutions, agencies, and public offices are mentioned, but the characters involved are wholly imaginary.

ISBN: 9798863658704

Some stories originally appeared in the following publications:
Juked, 3AM Magazine, Drunk Monkeys, Pacifica Literary Review, Fixional, Cheap Pop, Flash Fiction Press, Identity Theory, Horror Sleaze Trash, Straylight Literary Arts Magazine, Belletrist Magazine, The Birds We Piled Loosely, Red Fez, Weirderary, and *Two Cities Review*.

CONTENTS

8   *Before the Giant Anteater*

14   *George Washington Slept With a Psychic*

18   *Mega Walmart CEO President King*

28   *Your Man for a Prison*

35   *Baby Alice*

40   *Human Gauntlet*

45   *Jack, a Kind of First*

57   *Mike Went to Guam*

65   *Angelica*

69   *Caltrain Normcores*

74   *One Hang Up*

79   *Small Town Date Night*

- **85** *Territorial Pissings*
- **88** *Killer's Trance*
- **93** *Santa Cruz Sex Cult*
- **96** *Richard Dawkins by the Light of the Full Moon*
- **101** *Last Day as an Urban Legend*
- **105** *Bona Fide Formaldehyde*
- **115** *E-Therapy Girls*
- **126** *Mustard Sleeve*
- **128** *Superhero Vinchenzo*
- **130** *Hologram Free Zone*
- **136** *Tusks of Varaha*
- **139** *Orion's Tooth*
- **143** *Nationalist Sweetheart*
- **150** *Trophy #Jailbait*

155 *Ace Ventura, Sleepy Doomsday*

158 *Dr. Hologram*

170 *Parole Officer Pete*

172 *Meta with Dave*

175 *Southside Park*

181 *Sam's Hang Glider Dive Bombs*

BEFORE THE GIANT ANTEATER

*This story is dedicated to the anteater owned by Salvador Dali. I had the sincere honor to witness the anteater choke to death on a chocolate-covered raisin in Paris in 1971. Never have I been so greatly distressed. I very nearly turned a shade off-color, and my delicate mistress, with whom I was enjoying aperitifs, likewise did not know what to think, say, or do for several minutes. – **André Breton***

*

Salvador Dali sometimes found himself estranged from his own creative abilities. He would look at his toothbrush and his mind would freeze up. He would stare into the cloud-filled sky and only see what struck his eyeballs—nothing more, quite possibly something profoundly much less. Forcing his mind to wander, cries of Marco Polo would echo off the hilltops of Europe. Finally an image! A mental association at last! Coming into focus: a slice of bread.

There are some roads that lead to nowhere. Actually, there are a lot of them. Most of them are in Arkansas.

Not far outside Little Rock, a certain Dr. Bryson had operated a solo medical practice for 50 years. He only charged one American dollar for each patient. Everyone living within ten miles had a story of how the doctor had saved his or her life.

Sometimes you don't always get what you pay for. Sometimes you get a little more. At least, one would certainly hope so, after only paying a dollar for a new lease on life.

Salvador ended up on the doorstep of Dr. Bryson late one evening. He was feeling especially ragged and out of sync, to say the least, with his creative forces. For the past several weeks, he had seen nothing but slices of bread.

He didn't have any American dollars; all he had was a toothbrush.

The doctor seemed insulted. "It's only one hundred pennies," he pouted. But he accepted the toothbrush anyway—with a certain reserved dignity.

Sometimes you do get what you pay for. The doctor gave Salvador exactly a toothbrush's worth of medical advice.

"Okay, here you go," said the doctor, handing Salvador a sheet of paper.   "What's this?"

"Your prescription."

"But you haven't examined me yet."

"Excuse me," said the doctor, jingling some pennies in his pocket and briskly exiting.

Salvador might have understood the reason behind the doctor's gruff actions. But he still suffered from his strange malady. Whenever he tried to seriously put thoughts together, he only saw bread. Not even a loaf—just a slice. Suddenly the only thing he possessed in the world was this doctor's prescription. As far as he knew, it was the best medical advice of the day.

Examining the crucial scribble, Salvador recognized the name of a nearby establishment—a bar he had noticed on the road toward Little Rock. Twenty minutes later, he found himself ordering a whiskey sour. It was given to him on the house, in appreciation for his fancy French accent. His face was beat red and he felt distinctly hot under the collar. This situation could not have been anticipated. It was bikini bull riding night.

After a few quick gulps, Salvador regained his calm. He raised his eyes to the stage. Confidence came. Soon he began to enjoy himself.

Breasts, when you are really, genuinely, freely, and openly allowed to look at them, are quite healthy to the spirit. Under other circumstances, when you want to look but aren't allowed to, or aren't 100% sure how much trouble you might be in for if you go ahead and dare—then they can, instead, be quite damaging. The spirit sulks.

There wasn't much question about these Arkansonian girls' breasts. Loosely and lazily concealed in subtle bikini-wear, they were most certainly, really, genuinely, freely, and openly willing to be viewed. They also bounced up and down—as the girls bounced up and down—as the mechanical bull bucked between the girls' legs. Speaking at least for Salvador: the spirit soared.

When a girl's top came undone, everyone acted as if it was the last thing they had expected. They all went crazy. The girl squealed and tried to cover herself. Her breasts were bright and fun.

The topless girl's set concluded rather suddenly when an old man in the crowd keeled over. One man's medical treatment is another's heart attack. Someone in the crowd shouted to call the doctor. Immediately several generous souls donated their pennies to the cause.

A few more girls took the stage, one after the other. Salvador enjoyed a few more drinks. But soon he was just about ready to call it a night. He had seen some nice breasts. He felt alright. Now it was time for practical considerations. For instance, how was he supposed to brush his teeth?

It's very natural for the mind to begin wandering at a time like this. Breasts, whiskey, and no toothbrush. Salvador leaned against the bar, pressing his jawbone against his knuckle, crushing his pointed mustache. Considering the trifling wasteland of Arkansas, he mused about all the roads leading to nowhere.

"Hey," said an unusual, disembodied voice somewhere in his consciousness. "Hey, nobody's invited you, William Shakespeare. If you touch my girl one more time, I'll take your globe theatre and I'll tell you where to shove it."

It took a moment, but Salvador finally got a read on the speaker. His heart sank, as he figured it would just be another slice of bread. But then he saw: it was a giant anteater, scratching itself with a hind leg while stretching its snout around the plump behind of a young Quapaw Indian of the Ozarks. She was performing a slow-motion gourd dance and reciting Shakespeare sonnets. "And the counterfeit is poorly imitated after you; on Helen's cheek all art of beauty set, and you in Grecian tires are painted new."

*

Salvador Dali returned to Paris in 1968 with a singular companion, the giant anteater from the Ozarks. They lived joyously together in the abandoned tunnels of the Paris subway until 1971, when a certain chocolate-covered raisin lodged itself in the anteater's esophagus, leading to a lack of oxygen to the brain, and a speedy, somewhat violent and assuredly unpleasant death. The papers said it was a beetle, but I doubt that, unless it was heavily chocolate covered.

GEORGE WASHINGTON SLEPT WITH A PSYCHIC

George Washington slept with a psychic during his midlife crisis. She kept a vial of poison hemlock next to her bed.

"What happens if you have just a little?" he asked.

"I can't say from experience. Only from second hand sources," said Evelyn, the psychic. "There's some disagreement."

"Want to try some with me?"

Evelyn didn't usually sleep with her clients. She was worried about getting pregnant.

"Sure," she said.

The ghost of Caesar Augustus, one of her go-to sources for any number of questions, including hemlock consumption, rose up from the floor just then. It was a younger version of Augustus than the one portrayed in his famous bust. He was maybe twelve.

"Who's he?" Augustus asked.

"That's George Washington," the psychic answered.

George couldn't hear this exchange. Oblivious to the presence of the Roman emperor, he popped open the vial of hemlock and gave it a sniff.

"I think he's an idiot," Augustus stated proudly in Latin.

"Maybe so, but pretty soon he's going to be very important in world history."

"Does that mean he pays extra?"

"No. Right now he's practically a nobody. The war hasn't even started yet."

"With the Greeks?"

"The British."

"Sounds like a bunch of idiots."

"Maybe so, but he's going to solve the British problem. Right when the war breaks out, he's going to calm everyone down, convince the British to lower their taxes, and make everyone shake hands. Then, he's going to strengthen the fundamental pillars of democracy and give everyone the right to vote, including women."

"How exciting."

"For the first time ever, there will be world peace. And it will continue forever, or at least for as far as my crystal ball can see into the future."

"Hm."

"What? You're not impressed?"

"It sounds pretty bleak if you ask me."

George coughed hoarsely and gasped for breath.

"Are you okay, George?"

Unable to answer, he clutched his neck and began to spasm uncontrollably.

"What's this stuff?" Augustus asked, picking up the vial. He turned it upside down to show that it was empty.

"That's hemlock. I thought you were an expert with it."

"I'm twelve! I'm not an expert at anything!"

Evelyn was really looking forward to the United States. The colonies were crap. The British were pompous jerks. Besides, she wanted to get some predictions right for a change.

Augustus gave George a poke.

"I knew it. He's dead."

"That's not possible!" said Evelyn, consulting her crystal ball. "Look!"

The ball showed a world of peace and harmony, everyone laughing and getting along perfectly.

Not paying attention, twelve-year-old Augustus climbed inside George's dead body and made it sit up and look around.

"Hello," said the body, "my name is George and I make all the rules because I'm such a big part of world history!"

The psychic hardly noticed this performance. She was too engrossed in her crystal ball. Something seemed to be going wrong with the future. All the future world peace was turning into familiar chaos.

"Augustus?"

Evelyn suddenly noticed that Augustus had vanished and had taken George's body with him.

"George!" she cried, running for the door. But George was dead, she remembered; she corrected herself, "Augustus!!!"

The street outside was deserted. Somewhere out there, a world-domination-crazed twelve-year-old was running around in George Washington's body.

Evelyn hurried back to her crystal ball to see what would happen next.

MEGA WALMART CEO PRESIDENT KING

To visit Emmett, you need a flashlight. That's how you let him know you've arrived and you're ready for the rope. When he sees your signal, he tosses the rope over the side of the Mega Walmart and you climb right up the building.

Emmett lives on the Mega Walmart's roof—right on top of the epicenter of capitalism.

I flashed the light, making a certain pattern, just as an old heroin addict had instructed me to do. It was the guy's dying words. If you're homeless for a while, you know about Emmett; but you've got to hang around chronic overdosers if you ever want to learn how to visit him.

I flashed the light for about an hour before Emmitt noticed. Then down came the rope.

For a homeless guy, Emmett's really got it all. He's got all the latest electronics, camping supplies, cooking appliances... His clothes are always new and perfectly fitting and his shoes are always shiny.

On the roof we took a seat on a brand new rug and sipped good whisky from crystal tumblers. Emmett sat on a black leather office chair, just like a real business executive or somebody.

"Travel far?" he asked.

"Yeah, El Paso," I said.

"Train hopping mostly. Walking if we had to," said Sal, my traveling buddy.

We also had Corndog with us. Picked him up a few blocks away. He offered us some bargain meth, so we said he could pretend to be with us.

Sal provided the flashlight, but I was the only one who knew the correct signal and the address. There is quite the abundance of Mega Walmarts around these days, but there's only one with Emmett on top.

Emmett quizzed the hell out of us. He wondered mostly if we'd ever done any honest work. That's the thing that gets you cut out of the opportunity of a lifetime right away—if you've ever done even a day's honest work. If you have, then you've learned the value of things. You're corrupted. You can no longer appreciate the fruits of the garden as they were intended: free.

I was an easy pass. In terms of work, I'm a complete virgin.

Sal has a proudness about himself I knew might raise eyebrows. But I figured he'd be a go. You can see he's a full-bred lazy bagga bones from miles away.

Corndog was a gamble. Emmett gave him a short and sweet grilling. You could tell Emmett knew the score. Despite Corndog's lies, you could see he'd done some basic fast food work and maybe a bit of community service, which counts as labor, the poor bastard. But Emmett wasn't too big of a hard ass. To Corndog, he said, "You're a damn fraud, kid, but I know how you're probably playing smart to somehow benefit these true knights. I'll give you a one-time pass."

So far, Emmett was living up to his reputation. All those urban legends weren't shitting us. I felt like I would have gladly killed for this homeless, freeloading goddamn saint.

"Now," said Emmett, "I see you've come all this way. What is it that you want?"

"I don't know," I said. "Just the usual stuff I guess."

I could tell we were about to have our minds blown. How could I say exactly what I wanted? I was clearly too much of an idiot to know what I was missing in my life. I hoped Emmett would answer that one for me. But I could tell from his look that I'd said the wrong thing.

"Cigarettes, jerky, whiskey…" said Sal, always practical.

"Lube," said Corndog, the weirdo, probably thinking he was pretty damn funny.

"Come on," said Emmett. He led us to the center of the roof.

Right there in the exact middle of the Mega Walmart was a keypad inexplicably imbedded in the roof's surface.

Emmett punched in a code. Like some futuristic thing, a circular section of the roof silently opened up.

"Down there," he said, "is so much gum, so many cigarettes, and so much lube, you could spend your whole life doing nothing but indulging, and still there would be an endless supply. Now, think long and hard about what you want. I'm telling you, this is your chance to take it as it was meant to be: completely free."

Emmett tossed a rope through the hole in the roof and we shimmied down. We had the whole place to ourselves.

I've been to a few Mega Walmarts before, but always as a sort of tourist, restricted by the fact that I've never been the world's best thief. It felt pretty good knowing I could take anything—like it was already mine. This wasn't the first time I'd felt this way. But now I felt justified, like I wasn't some kind of outcast or plague on society.

"One hour," said Emmett. "Then meet back here. Don't be late or the alarm will sound."

It was dark—dark in an intentional way, like a haunted house. There were a few neon exit signs and other random light sources that made everything only just visible.

Between myself, Sal, and Corndog...we didn't even give each other a second glance before we each headed off in our own separate missions.

Wandering into the darkness, I quickly became lost in the maze of aisles. I was hanging out in the candy section when I heard a scream from across the store. I figured I'd just eat a few Snickers first, then investigate. There was more yelling and a bunch of shelves crashed down, shit breaking, etc.

Sensing something was up, I crept over to the men's apparel section. I heard a moaning sound from the corner. That's where I found Sal: gagged and tied up to a display of boxer shorts.

I had only been in Walmart for fifteen minutes and I kept discovering all kinds of new things I needed. Now I had to add boxers to the list.

"What happened?" I asked, undoing Sal's gag.

Just then I was jumped from behind, knocked to the ground, and hit over the head. Next thing I knew, I was tied up in the electronics department.

"Okay, you're awake," said Corndog. "I thought maybe you were dead or something."

I was gagged pretty tight or else I would have yelled for help.

Corndog stood there like a punk ready for a serious scuffle. In addition to the baseball bat in his hands, he had a bunch of guns, hunting knives, and survival gear strapped to his body.

"I'm taking over this Walmart," he said. "From now on, it's mine."

All the guns and knives started to make sense. I never figured a guy named Corndog could be so ambitious.

"I'm currently recruiting a second in command. I might choose to incorporate as a monarchy, in which case the open position is duke. Otherwise it might be vice president. I was going to offer the position to Sal, but he called me an ungrateful piece of shit while I was binding him up. So, I'll offer the position to you instead."

"What about Emmett?"

"I don't trust him."

"Is he tied up, too?"

"I can't find him. He disappeared. But at the top of the hour, we all know where he'll be. If he protests, this Walmart shotgun will make things right."

"How much does the position pay?"

Isn't this what you're supposed to ask when considering a job offer? I'd never worked before, but I wasn't going to start now unless I could get some reasonable compensation, considering the life skills and abilities I have to offer.

"Sure," he said. "You can take one food thing for every hour you work and one non-food thing for every five hours. That's as good as it gets. All other employees will get a minimum stipend of pre-opened goods."

He untied me.

"Thanks, Corndog," I said.

"That's King Corndog from now on, buddy," he said. "Or President Corndog."

"Is president the same as CEO?"

"I think so. Whichever is more important, that's what I am."

"I've never met a CEO before."

"Shut up."

Corndog patted me down to see if I had any weapons. I only had a bunch of Snickers.

"I'll take these out of your first day's salary," he said. "Now, it's your job to secure all the doors. I'm going to go see about setting up cameras on the outside and a few battle stations throughout the kingdom. When the cleaning staff shows up in the morning, I'll try to recruit some so we won't have to clean up after ourselves."

The doors looked pretty secure to me. Then again, they could use a little extra securing, since they were only made out of glass. I tried to be enthusiastic. We were entering a whole new era of Walmart security with me at the helm as Corndog's vice president. I pushed a few magazine displays over the doors and called it good.

Not that I was too sure how serious to take any of this. Just to be on the safe side, I went to the hunting section and loaded up on my own artillery and battle equipment. Then I made a secret stash of gum, cigarettes, and Snickers just so I'd never have to worry about affording any of my favorite things.

With about fifteen minutes till the top of the hour, I went back to the men's underwear section.

Sal was gone.

"Sal?" I said, not too loud, peaking around all the underwear racks.

If I knew my buddy Sal, he'd be needing a drink right about now. Lucky for him, Mega Walmarts stalk just about every major brand of everything—even some of the top shelf stuff.

By the time I walked to the alcohol section, it was five minutes till the hour. No Sal. I helped myself to some Jack Daniels.

The whole place was eerily quiet. All the overflowing shelves were starting to get on my nerves. If this were all mine, I wouldn't really give a shit. I'd probably give everything away. I guess that probably means I'd make a lousy worker. Go figure.

I had a sudden urge to destroy everything. I had to restrain myself. Then again, this place, as a whole, was pretty unbreakable. Mega Walmarts don't burn and it would take forever to break everything one by one. The destructive urge began to fade. Jack Daniels helped.

Now feelin pretty good, I made my way back to the center of the store.

"Psst!" It was Sal by the board games.

"Hey!" I said in a whisper. "Been looking for you!"

Sal was all loaded up with artillery, too.

"Who would have thought Corndog would screw us over like that? You know he tried to make me some kind of vice president? Fuck that guy! We got to hunt him down."

I glanced at my hunting watch. It was exactly the top of the hour.

"We should go see about Emmett," I said. "That's where Corndog is going to be."

"Is that what he said? What else did he tell you?"

"I don't know."

"He's such a prick! I swear to god when I see him, he's dead!"

When we got to the center of the Mega Walmart, all we saw was an old guy in a janitor's suit mopping up the tile. Getting closer, we saw it was Emmett.

"Got everything you need?" he asked.

Sal and I exchanged an awkward glance. Each of us were loaded down with guns and knives, nothing else.

"Had some trouble with your friend Corndog," Emmett continued. "It happens sometimes. Guys like him help keep my night crew staffed."

Climbing up the rope to the roof, I spotted Corndog in the distance, a chain around his neck, mopping up by the lingerie. I knew more strongly than ever I never wanted to work a day in my life. I shuddered at the thought and regretted ever having considered becoming vice president or duke of a Mega Walmart. On the roof, Sal and I shed our weapons. We left empty-handed.

YOUR MAN FOR A PRISON

It's been about a year since I got into the prison selling biz. Sold my first prison to a toothless guy with family money. Said he'd use it to lock up dentists. Guy had no use for dentists. Not the first thing I'd do with a prison, but hey, I don't use 'em. I just sell 'em.

Got one up on the market now. Don't know why anyone would pass it up. It's got all the basics: 700 cells, four shower rooms, a kitchen (appliances come as-is), a long-hall cafeteria, and a half-acre yard with a full basketball court.

Think about this. After your dinner party with all your elite-class buddies, you can liven things up with a sweaty game of ball. If you keep score, you can lock up the losers. Now that sounds like a fun night and a good use of a prison if you ask me!

*

"Bob, you're the flyer guy, right?"

"That's me."

"Take a look at this. Tell me you wouldn't buy this prison, huh?"

Bob, the lucky dog, sells courthouses. He's the flyer guy, too—can make a dazzler of a flyer in no time. Sells those old courthouses like they were the year's hot item. Guess they probably are at this point.

"No, don't think I need any prisons today. Nice flyer, though."

"Come on, Bob, I'll trade you a prison for a courthouse. Square trade and you can even keep the flyer."

Old Bob just laughed.

"I mean, Bob, think about it. You can fit twelve of your stuffiest courthouses in this one historic landmark of a prison."

Bob just kept laughing. He handed back the flyer and returned to his work, making courthouse sales receipts.

What the hell. Don't even know why I bother, some days.

Storming out of the office, I nearly bowled Jen right over.

"Hey! Where you off to so early?" she asked. She sells grade schools and sometimes community parks. No way she understands my troubles.

"Off to go find more happy customers with no teeth!"

*

We go about this business as if there's still some real use for these rotting government buildings. Everybody knows there's not. And they're overpriced as hell. Unless your favorite thing is hiring wrecking crews.

The government buyout was a good day. But you can't let the old structures just take up space and decay. So some genius at the top had the stellar insight to sell them off and let other private jerks deal with the hassle of repurposing. Makes sense unless you're thinking in particular about prisons. How can you repurpose a prison? Good luck!

Right now Jen's back at the office getting debriefed by Bob. She's asking why I've been so up tight. Bob's telling her in his special tone of "What, you mean you haven't heard?" Yeah, the monthly reports are due tomorrow. And Buddy, your man for a prison, hasn't sold any prisons. What about his sale to the guy with the dentist thing? "What, you mean you haven't heard?" Yeah, even that's up in the air. Dentist Hater, despite his many great qualities—he prob ain't good for the check. Credit a mess. Assets a joke. Sad but true.

*

Had no choice but to hit up the old police stations. Even though common knowledge is that they're infested by all the ex-con types. Ex-cons playing ex-cops. Not exactly a shrewd business model, guys. Nobody making any money. They just get angrier every day.

First police station I stopped off at, sure enough, peered through the window to find a group of shaved-head dudes. All in jumpsuits. I took a deep breath. Do you know what you can do with fifteen percent of the sale price of a prison? You can do a lot, that's what. In my case, you can pay off loans. Then, you can pay off more loans. And eventually, you can become solvent and talk first thing to Mandy, who sells houses in the best, neatest, cleanest districts where all the neighbors are peace-loving, upstanding anarchists championing stable employment.

"Hey, fellas!" I said, entering the police station. "Sorry for bustin in on ya, but—!"

Next thing, they had me pinned to the wall with a knife to my neck and gun to my head.

"Are you a cop?!" they demanded.

"Cop? How could I be a cop?" I said, almost laughing. "There are no cops anymore!"

"What do you mean no cops?" They asked. "This is a cop station! We took it over!"

"I see that!"

It didn't seem there was an apparent leader in the group. They didn't take turns yelling threats, just yelled all at once. You're dead! I'ma gonna kill you! Shove this knife down your face! Fuckin bullet in your brains!

"Easy guys, I'm just a realtor! God damn!"

First came a real-life punch to my jaw. Then a knee to my ribs. Then I was pummeled—it was like, game on! And it didn't let up. It didn't stop.

*

I came to. Barely conscious, knowing very little. But my mind gathered enough info from my swollen eyes and numb ears to form an association having to do (of course) with prisons. My first real thought was that I prob needed to quit my job as soon as possible. I was getting prisons on the brain. Not what I'd consider healthy.

Tried to move. Well, that didn't work out! Aches all over. Bones broken? Neck...in a brace? Tried to open the ol' jaw. Couldn't. But it was like my mouth was open already?

Prisons! I thought... Prisons!

Something moved. According to my rudimentary awareness. Naturally it was something in a white coat. Prison guard.

I drifted away.

*

Eventually I woke up again. I was, in fact, in a prison cell, strapped to a chair, surrounded by dentists. Not prison guards—dentists. A small discrepancy. I was fully conscious by this point. The dentists were all gathered around, working as a team on every square millimeter of my mouth and busted jaw.

I had a visitor. Nobody I knew. He introduced himself as one of the loan people. He said I owed them an awful lot of money (no kidding). Also he said they'd been trailing me for a while, trying to figure out how to get assets out of me (not an easy thing!). When they saw me getting pulverized by a gang of ex-cons, they jumped in to save the day (thanks a lot! I guess!). Since I couldn't afford any proper medical care, they brought me to this place, which they now owned, since the guy who bought it went bankrupt after all.

The loan guy left with a bill. It included my life's worth of debts plus the expense of having saved my life. Life-saving services, apparently...not cheap!

*

"Ah, you're awake," said one of the dentist inmates the next time I came around. "Just finishing up jaw surgery round three. Your colleagues were here visiting a moment ago to check on you. You were still under, so... But they left a card and some flowers. Would you like me to read it to you?"

"Huh, huh," I moaned, meaning, "God, no!" But the dentist didn't take the hint.

"'Dear Buddy,'" he read, "'sorry to hear about the monthly figures. Tough situation. Everybody's on your side, even management I hear. Too bad it's just a numbers thing. Darn it. But ever need a flyer for future employment reasons, or what have you, you know who to call. Bob.' And Jen says, 'I'm so sorry, Buddy! They'll fix you right up! I know they will! Don't let this hold you back ever, okay? You'll get out of there somehow! I know you will! You'll always be the man for a prison!'"

BABY ALICE

Baby Alice came out with an infected head. She was five pounds, atheist, vegan, and spoke a combination of English and Russian, as requested by forms 91-6A, 93-B1, and 78-L9 respectively. The infected head, which was not requested, had caused a massive purple bulge to form between the left eye and ear.

"No milk!" Alice screamed in her first words when a white-mustached doctor came with a needle. "I'm vegan!"

"Shhh..." said the doctor. "Holds still, Alice. It's only to kill the pain."

Baby Alice cursed at the doctor in Russian. Her voice was husky and authoritative, as per form 88-P2.

"I know my rights," said Alice, crying now.

The doctor laughed. This kid was making good use of her vocab module, all right.

"We're just draining all the puss out," the nurse explained, leaning in with a large syringe.

There was about a pint of puss. It was bright yellow and incredibly warm.

"What should I do with this, doctor?" asked the nurse. The doctor gave some orders under his breath. The nurse nodded. All very solemn, Baby Alice noticed.

"No!" she said. "Give it back!"

"Shhhh…" the doctor cooed, poking the baby with a strong sedative.

"You won't get away with this…!" But before she could even get out a single curse in Russian, she was out cold.

When Baby Alice awoke, she was alone in her hospital room. She could hear her mother out in the hall talking with the nurse. Still in her very first moments of life, Alice sized up her mom as a sweet but gullible woman. A product of a time before form 91-6A, etc.

The nurse was saying, "She's doing very well. She's resting now…"

There were footsteps leading away. Then silence.

"Yeah right, those bastards," said Alice, jumping out of bed and doing a summersault to the door (kinesthetic hyper-enrichment per form 61-B2).

The white-mustached doctor was standing huddled behind a desk with a couple of other quacks. In undertones, they were discussing the success of the day's harvest. Alice crept up close to listen.

"Another eight gallons today. That's fifteen gallons since Sunday."

"My god, it's a goldmine!"

A look of extreme fury crossed Alice's face. When the doctors had their backs turned, she whizzed past. Putting her hyper sensitive nose into action, she sniffed out the trail of puss in the air, following it to a locked door. With no time to lose, she kicked it right down.

"You think Alice is okay?" asked her mom to her dad a short distance down the hall.

"We paid so much extra for those super abilities and genetic corrections, she damn well better pull through!"

"Imagine an infection on her head. Never heard of that, have you?"

"I don't like the sound of it..." her dad grumbled.

Entering the locked room, Baby Alice closed the busted door and gasped. The room was filled with hanging bags of baby head puss. There must have been hundreds of them.

Just then... "What happened to the door?" It was the doctor's voice. His head poked into the room.

Alice panicked. She was standing right in the open holding a dozen bags of baby puss.

What was this stuff anyway? That was the great mystery. They were harvesting it for something.

"Hey!" yelled the doctor, storming towards Alice.

Not quite old enough to restrain her baby impulses (despite her better judgment as per form 23-BL), Alice ripped open one of the bags and guzzled the puss.

"What are you doing you crazy baby?!"

The doctor began backing away, terrified. Baby Alice burped, muttered something in Russian, and got a little wobbly. Her eyes began to water. She turned red and broke into a burning sweat.

It was only then that she realized that this, her first meal, didn't exactly satisfy her vegan ideals. So that was one mistake. Also she suddenly found herself seriously questioning her convictions as a born and bred atheist. It was like her whole life up to this point had been a sham. For a whole seven hours, she had been living in a fantasy world of lies and evil deceptions. But now her eyes were open and she saw the truth—not only that there was a god, but that she herself was god.

"Out of my way!" she bellowed and her voice was huskier and more authoritative than ever. She raced around the hospital curing everyone and punching anybody who got in her way.

When the god juice/baby puss began to wear off, doubts immediately crept in. Her pre-programmed atheism was triggered like a switch. Also she was hungry and dying for a real vegan meal, served on the bosom of her half English half Russian momma.

Exhausted, Baby Alice stumbled back into her hospital room and started crying in her bed. She didn't even notice the new purple bulge that was beginning to grow on the side of her head...

At last she fell asleep and the doctors, one by one, peaked into her room. When it was determined that it was safe to enter, the white-mustached doctor escorted her parents to her bedside. In her troubled dreams, Baby Alice could hear her father's voice demanding an answer.

"We're harvesting it..." the doctor whispered, "for aliens...for the government...for god..."

HUMAN GAUNTLET

He'd been up in Chico getting medical treatments for several years. Before long, he was just another midtown scene-kid who'd moved on (people in Sacramento were always leaving for San Francisco, LA...). He was forgotten, for the most part—except whenever a group got together and ate pizza with psilocybin mushrooms.

I grew up religious, so none of this seemed too weird to me. If you know what it's like to pray every night and actually feel something there, then you know how any shit you want can become real if you keep a line of communication open. You send signals out there, sure enough you'll get something back.

Several years is a long time to get medical treatments. No one knew what sort. All the better. Ideally his life was in the balance. We could only speculate how his medical team was a group of spiritual quacks, herbalists, and drug dealers.

"I saw Dante last night," someone would say. They'd say, "He was in the shape of a wild boar." They'd say, "I heard his voice in the train whistle. He was the train going by." They'd say, "I saw his ghost. He's dead."

It's like Schrodinger's cat. You put Dante in medical treatment in Chico; for as long as he stays in Chico, he occupies two realities. He's both dead and alive. It can't be confirmed either way, but it can't be neither.

When you see him alive, he's alive.

When you see him dead, he's dead.

According to quantum mechanics, he's in a super position. He's not one thing or another until someone looks. So far, no one has peeked into Chico. We've only got these mushroom trip visions. They go either way.

Chico is a dead town. A dead, bro, dusty town. From Sacramento, it's only an hour and a half away. You could sleep in and still drive there and back by noon.

All of us secretly doubted that, though. The way we figured it, if we drove there, we'd get sucked in. We'd never come back.

As far as Schrodinger's cat is concerned, it's not that simple. The cat was just in a box waiting to be either killed or not killed at random. In Chico, Dante was receiving medical treatment. Doubtless his life was in the balance. At the same time, you could bet he was somehow transforming himself.

A few summers ago, right around the time he left for Chico, I ran into Dante at Espresso Metro, the filthy little coffee shop at Sac City College. He was in a corner drinking coffee and staring at a girl with her blouse tied in a knot at her belly button. I sat down and said hey. He kept staring at the girl, then looked at me. He was there to sell a mushroom bag. That's what I figured since he was wearing his pizza uniform. He'd been fired from the pizza place months before, but he never returned the uniform and still wore it for drug deals.

"I failed the human gauntlet," he told me. There was meaning in this. He was on the mushrooms. I said a few things but he didn't respond. The girl he'd been looking at got up and left. He just kept saying, "I failed the human gauntlet."

He must have said that about ten times before I noticed that the side of his head was all bloody. His grungy look made it hard to tell, but after noticing it once, it was obvious: his long, dark hair was definitely matted with blood. I looked more closely and also saw that he was hiding a black eye under his sunglasses. His shirt was torn in several places. His posture was off, as if something was wrong with his spine. Casually glancing under the table, I saw his bare legs were wrapped in bloody gauze at the knees.

I was late for class so I had to rush away. It was the last time I ever saw him.

"I failed the human gauntlet," he said, staring down at his bloody hands.

Years passed and I was still working on my associates degree. It was my fifth year at community college. My life was not moving on.

One night, I ordered a large pizza all for myself. I was supposed to be studying for my midterm exams, but I didn't feel like it. What's the use of an associates degree anyway? I figured I'd just eat pizza, get fat, and drop out. I also had a small bag of mushrooms. I'd been saving them for exactly this sort of night.

Around 1 a.m. I started having visions. There were all kinds of religious undertones. That's not much of a surprise given the way I grew up. I figured I'd start to really feel something any second now, the way I used to when I'd pray every night before bed. More beautiful and pure and true than anything. I felt it coming on.

The sun rose at some point during my visions—and I guess I must have been asleep. I was outside along the side of an empty street. Nothing around me looked familiar.

It took me over an hour to figure out where I was, although to this day I don't know what the hell happened. I was in Chico. Of course I was. I was in goddamn Chico.

First thing I did was to walk to a coffee shop. It was a longshot, but I'd heard that Dante's brother worked at the place. I had never met the guy, but I recognized him immediately. I introduced myself.

"Is Dante around?" I asked.

"No," said the brother. "He's gone."

"Gone?" I blurted. It was like he might as well have said "dead." I asked, "Where did he go?"

The brother finished pulling an espresso shot. I could tell he was hungover and didn't want to talk. Also I sensed he was suspicious of me. But he finally told me anyway.

"He moved to Hillsboro—up by Portland—about a year ago. He works for a mattress supply company as a delivery guy."

I nodded, not quite understanding, and took my coffee outside. It was already warm out, even though it wasn't even 9 a.m. And the place was a dump alright. A wasteland. The exact opposite of the bohemian paradise we tried to create in the Victorian attics of Sacramento. It was enough to crush my soul at a single glance. Goddamn Chico. I've been stuck here ever since.

JACK, A KIND OF FIRST

Jack's dad promised enough wedding money to creep out Jesus. How much could an auto mechanic care about his transgender daughter's marriage to a singer on food stamps? Enough to make that pot belly of his suck in until he birthed five paychecks, I guess.

But then he caught wind of my excitement. Just like that, he wanted to back out like the jerk I figured he was from the start.

"Let it go," said Jack, her pretty face sad with terrible makeup. I could sense her frustration with my over-eagerness.

"Could, but not gonna," I said.

"I don't want him there anyway. He'll ruin it."

"I love me some ruined things."

"You know there are different classes of ruined things. This is a ruined thing like food you can't eat. It's no good."

"But ruined food, you just puke it up!"

"I hate puking."

"No way! When was the last time you puked? It's like primo catharsis. Especially if you really might die if you don't. One second you're poisoned to death for sure, then you're retching your guts out all over the place in a spontaneous letting go as intense as gravity calling it quits, or whatever. Then suddenly you feel like a million bucks."

"Well, there is the money…"

"It's worth a frickin shot, babe."

*

The second you see yourself having troubles with love, you know you can't go away empty handed. Love in the normal sense requires giving. But in times of crisis, it's time to take! Just like lawyers live and breathe this, I've been training.

*

Jack tried playing in my band but that didn't work out. Then she showed up at a Wiccan full moon dance and we drank wine out of the same gourd. It spilled all over her shirt and her new implants looked stellar. Next day she was at a coffee shop hung over and I asked if she'd marry me.

"Dad's still paying off my surgeries and I haven't told him the details. He thinks it was knee surgery."

"Don't you know who I am?"

"Sure. I tried out for your band, remember?"

"Dude, I mean, don't you know what I do?"

"No."

"Okay, I'm the guy who gets married once a year—trying to break the world record for marriages and all that shit. They wrote about it in the paper and a few lawsuits make it extra culturally relevant. I'm kind of a big deal when it comes to the marriage biz."

She gave me queer looks. Gave me that scowl with the "aw come on" eyes.

"I mean fuck your dad," I said. "Getting married is a huge sham!"

"Sounds like with you it is."

"Totally the opposite. With me it's the greatest. It's a blast. I'm the only thing happening in modern relationships today."

"So why me?"

"It's not everyone who drinks wine from gourds."

"Ever married a trans chick before?"

"Transvestite once."

"How'd that go?"

"Same as all the others."

"Good?"

"Humans are the best! Don't you just want to marry all of them?"

"Even that guy?"

Some cranky bastard a few tables away. Dressed in the shambles of normcore. Sitting at his computer Googling "rocks" with a clear hard on.

"Hell yeah!" I said.

"Don't."

I went over to the guy. Leaned on his table.

"You like rocks?" I asked.

"Yes," he answered, smug as hell.

"God, me too. Want to get married?"

*

Slowly dying with cancer in a hospital but at least you've got the nursing staff. All your guts in the street after a car crash but look at all the party lights of everyone coming to the rescue. Silently at night going with your arms wrapped around your younger wife, fast asleep. (What are people even thinking when they promise love eternal?) Shot in an alley by a chump on crack and you just wish he'd got your head and not your damn groin.

*

Doing this thing right means all the full ceremony my backyard just can't offer. Melissa had to wear a plastic wedding gown as a last minute invention. Sarah had to settle for a plain chocolate box cake instead of her dream of marijuana brownies for everyone. She also wanted more of a wedding bed than my blow-up mattress.

"Hey girl," I said, "It's no crime being poor! It just sucks but we'll get by!"

She got pregnant by some other prick while we were still married just to hurt me. I saved up, talked my dealer down, and sent weed brownies to the baby shower.

With Jack: we picked a date and settled on the park by the water. Had some elaborate schemes for catering and entertainment. Began to research all the best wedding rituals dreamed up by pagan cultures. Jack talked up her Wiccan buddies for ideas. We made certain the stars were properly aligned for the next full moon.

*

"Shouldn't we wait till our wedding night?" Jack asked, face down on my bed.

"That goes against my only true virtue: not procrastinating."

"But just in this case—for the full moon, ya know?"

"You're shy!"

"No!"

"Damn, you are! I knew it! Come on, take your panties off."

"I hate that word!"

"What, panties? Panties, panties, panties!"

She ran up against the wall, looking around for something to bash me with.

"It has nothing to do with the wedding..." I said, crazy soft when she expected screams.

"What do you mean?"

"If we just do it after the wedding, then it's just another part of the stupid ass ceremony I want to destroy anyway."

"Just not right now, okay?"

"Ah, come on," I pressed against her, but she slipped loose, grabbing her bag, ready to walk out.

"It's okay for me to say no."

"I can say no, too, and see how you like it."

"Oh yeah?"

"No, no, no."

*

She came back the next night. Immediately asked for a beer and asked what I was up to.

"Right now? Researching some fine points for my lawsuits. Pretty exhilarating and shit. Legal system's fucked up."

"Okay, well let's make a deal."

"Sure."

"Let me in your band and we can do it."

I stood up. Had a sip of beer. Thought it over.

"And you'll let me say panties?"

"No. that's going too far. But you can take them off."

"Okay, you got it, babe. It's a deal."

*

Played a knockout show a few weeks later and introduced our new bassist as my future wife. All my ex wives in the crowd went nuts like a real bunch of groupies.

First thing if you ever want to set the record for the world's most marriages, definitely start a rock band. Then marry a band manager. Then a booking agent. Then a chick to make your bros jealous while you get your glam shots and album covers made.

Then marry all your fans so at least you'll have people to add to your guest list when you've been on tour for five years and your tunes still blow.

Check, check, and check.

Sometime along the line, might as well marry a bassist while you're at it.

*

No one gets society. The core of it is purely primordial for one thing. The rest of it is either random or based on somebody else's vision of an ideal. All of it is off its nuts and basically just about sex and trying for all it's worth to keep this marriage thing working. Everyone's walking around thinking, "How can we protect this marriage thing at all costs?" Great question!

*

That's when Jack's dad waivered. Seems he looked me up. Could just picture the expression on his face (I looked him up, too) when he read about my lawsuits in the news. "Serial marrier makes mockery of traditional values. Hide your daughters!"

He wanted to know what the hell he was paying for if this thing wasn't going to be forever.

"Let's go talk to him."

Jack was worried. "What would you say?"

"Nothin. He'd just see I'm a nice, kindhearted kid, ya feel?"

"He liked guys with..."

"What, trust funds?"

"Family values."

"Oh wow. Okay, you're right, I might be out of luck with that. I don't even know where you get those."

*

How do you unlock the key to a mechanic's heart? You take your car in for a tune up, duh!

Good thing my sweet ride's got hella complex issues. You could diagnose the shit out of it and still find bugs in its engine pipes, dry-rot in the carburetor for days.

It was the earliest I'd gotten up in a decade and my nice kid face was struggling. But what's a mechanic, after all, if not another fellow human needing love?

"It's a real pleasure, Mr. Fry," I said almost genuinely when we met at the auto shop.

He eyed me like some kind of tax collector but shook my hand. I could tell he wanted to ignore that this was happening and get right on with the day's grease and gaskets.

"I'm Lucian," I said. "Friend of Jack's."

"When I heard Jack was getting married…"

He was all worked up. Couldn't express himself except to get red in the face. A man of few words! I shuffled my feet and waited for him to continue. I waited as long as possible.

"But anyway," I said finally, "my car here, it's got some noise it's making, plus it just hardly gets started and barely goes anymore. Think it's the breaks? The accelerator…?"

That's all it took to get him back in action. Dude's alright. He said a few things in mechanic speak and we were back in business. The trusty commerce game. In this together, we both stood there trying to wrap our brains around the issues of this rusty old junkheap.

*

Everything fell into place. The stars, the moon, even the money. We had enough alright. More than I'd ever seen in one place, for sure.

"Nervous, babe?"

"No."

"Is that a sad no or a shy no?"

"I don't know."

We were standing in a large circle of friends, ex wives, and Wiccans. The full moon was out like a sterile, loving hospital light.

"Your pop's here in spirit."

"He disowned me."

"Don't say that!"

"He did."

"The surgeries?"

"No. I told him about my surgeries. He didn't..."

"So it was the wedding?"

"Yes."

"Oh... Figured that might happen, when he wouldn't pay for it."

"Didn't he?"

"Sold my car. It wasn't worth a dime except for the stereo, which was frickin' priceless."

Jack teared up. My ex wives took notice and teared up, too. The Wiccans played along and began to wail and sob, tossing back swigs of wine by the gourdfull. In the center of this hot-blooded frenzy, we carried out our pagan rituals in silence.

*

Woke up in the woods in the early dawn with a Wiccan on either side. That's the great thing about being intoxicated. You can just say fuck it. I shivered and pulled the Wiccans closer.

"Jack's gone!" said a panicked voice in the back of my mind.

"Big deal," shrugged the rest of me. "Check out all my Wiccan palls, still good practically naked girls if ever I've seen any."

That was the party of parties, alright. People would be talking about the horrors and elations of that wedding day for years to come. Only I wouldn't know how Jack felt about it. I knew she wouldn't show up to the courthouse later, wouldn't sign the papers, wouldn't make it official. In the eyes of the law, we wouldn't be married. But at least the Wiccans would count it. Wouldn't they?

"Jack!" I yelled in my half asleep mind. "What do you say, Jack? Does it count?"

MIKE WENT TO GUAM

Mike went to Guam about the same time I converted to the Baha'i Faith. Mike would kick my ass if he knew, but right now he's too busy fixing broken down air conditioning units in Micronesia.

The ass-kicker friend is somebody we all need to keep close in our lives. Or in this case: keep far off in Guam but think of often.

Haven't talked to Mike in maybe 10 years. Thing is, he keeps me around as his faithful stalker friend. Everybody needs one of those, too. They keep track of you even when you're way off your mark, gone to seed, fucked for life.

—Not quite, your friendly stalker knows. You've still got that spark threading through. That bit of your early potential still hanging on. Mike can thank me for that later.

I grew up with religion—parents breathing Jesus down my neck. I met Mike right after his first trip to Guam. He was Jehovah's Witness and had visited the Guam village Dededo as a missionary. I know because he showed me pictures and explained how this made him an exemplary candidate for the "little flock"—the people who go to heaven, as opposed to the "other sheep."

In senior year's Contemporary Issues class, we'd yell at each other from across the room. (Back then, I could really see the benefits of Reconstructionism. You can look that shit up on your own time if you don't already know about it. Real sickos love it. It's fire and brimstone. Ancient God's harshest laws made into modern laws. Stone thieves, gays, and adulterers! That kind of thing.)

I'd stand on top of my desk and yell: "If God said this shit, then we've all got to wake the hell up! Swallow it, like it or not!"

And Mike would charge at me like a bull. He'd yank my desk out from under me.

"Idol worshiper!" he'd yell, really trying to pick a fight.

It's hard growing up with strong convictions.

"False prophet!" he'd scream.

"God will see about that!" I'd scream back, matching him shove for shove.

The other students circled around to cheer us on or just to laugh. The teacher was Catholic, so all he wanted was for us protestant boys to eat each other alive.

I knew that Mike was brainwashed pretty bad. Only knowing and thinking things he'd been instructed to know or think. But my radicalism was fresh, as I saw it, since I had just read the Bible and I took it to the absolute extreme—even more so than my puritanical parents.

"Don't water down the truth!" I said pretty often. "No gray areas!" I really hated the idea of gray areas.

I got over religion completely after graduation. Forgot about Mike, too. Except in the back of my mind when I needed someone to kick my ass.

Then stalking became my thing.

When you no longer have God everywhere in your life, you have to fill that "omnipotent eye watching over you" role somehow. Why not use the only person you know who will kick your ass for doing or saying the wrong thing? That's Mike.

When I'd be doing lots of drugs or fucking lots of babes, he'd pop into my head.

"Fornicator! Horrible waste of a life! Dumb druggie! Idiot!" I'd hear him yell and scream.

I'd have to follow his movements pretty closely to see what he thought was good or bad. Otherwise I'd just be shooting in the dark. It's what happens naturally when you move away from Reconstructionism. You don't have rules written in stone for you. All you have are man's laws. Mike's laws.

Keeping up with Mike was like keeping up with God on a cosmic downward spiral. He was always one step ahead of me. First with the girls. He'd be fucking them all over the place. Guys, too, probably. Anything he could fit his penis into. I can imagine how God must fuck just about everything. I picked that up pretty naturally.

There were quite a few impregnations all up and down the West Coast. A few in Mexico. I read about them daily in Mike's posts online. He had a blog called Total Fucking Piety. I'd read that daily while keeping up with his social media updates.

He was really on to something. By the time his women difficulties started to bring him down, he was already soaring back up in a path of ultra drunkenness. Every day he'd stumble down the street to the corner liquor store to buy a few bottles of whiskey. Which he would drink alone and dream—while his real life dreams and aspirations slipped away.

Luckily, I also had a liquor store right down the street. I wasn't as quick with the habit, but about a year into heavy drinking I could down a few bottles in a day. Success!

It had gotten to that point again. I listened to his yelling in the back of my head all day long.

Especially as I crawled home from the liquor store with a new batch of booze.

Now that was living! It had again reached that razor's edge. There was silence from his blog and his social media for awhile and I was despairing daily, a slave to the hard stuff. For sure, it wasn't just booze, either. Not by this point. There were also the drugs. All kinds. Pills, crack, crystal meth, weed…

Then he reemerged. I was all over his new posts. It was the only thing still alive for me—the only thing keeping me alive. God's voice!

Tell me how to live, Mike!

His latest venture: Politics. Revolution. Leading the people. Gaining a following. Liberating their souls. Laying down the sacred truths.

Drinking whole gallons of whiskey and smoking mountains of crack, I started to get pretty down on myself each time I read a new post. If Mike knew I was still wallowing in the drugs, he'd kick my ass.

"Drunk! Loser! I'll kick your ass!!!"

So one day I didn't go down to the liquor store. Also I didn't pick up my drug prescriptions from my local "got you covered" bro. After a few weeks passed, there I was, lying around in the dark, paranoid, ready to take on any new goddamn strong convictions, no matter what.

How was it going for Mike leading the people? Take a guess. It was going freaking great!

Next question: How was I not getting in on this?!

Followers, cool rituals, you can make up your own chants, people give you money. You give speeches and people really listen.

Like Mike, I started out on the street. Going around yelling.

"You think you're free? You're not! Want something better? Take a pamphlet!" Like that.

"Think you're living your life right? What a joke!" I could go on like this all day.

Before long, I had a group of a few hundred people signed up for my weekend retreat. I pieced together a holy man's outfit (robe, beard, sandals). I was all set.

Didn't prepare a speech. Figured I'd wing it. Then I'd just have everyone meditate for a while until I thought of something else to do.

From everybody's donations, I rented out a warehouse and some crates for a stage and a PA system for cheap. Also snacks, t-shirts for everyone. The whole deal.

The night of the opening ceremony, I had to get good and drunk to get my nerves in order. Then I went around and picked out a bunch of girls to bang after my big speech. Without that to look forward to, I'd never make it through this, I told myself.

Pulled it off pretty smoothly, I have to say. Always knew I had it in me. Ever since Contemporary Issues class when I shoved Reconstructionist crap down everyone's throats.

Not sure all I talked about. Except for getting all truthful and telling my followers all about Mike. "He's God in human form!" I explained. And I told them how he'd yell at me in my mind. Like, "You fucking idiot!"—and how useful that is, to have a real ass kicker for your god figure.

And I told them about how enlightening it is to stalk someone.

"Here's his blog I read everyday!" I said. "Here's his email, his phone number, and all his social media usernames! Also, in case you ever need it, here's his home address!"

It was about this time in my speech that Mike started yelling at me pretty unforgivingly.

"You're a fraud!" He yelled. "A hack! A phony! A shitty imposter! No one will ever believe you! No one! You're finished!"

Freaked out, I backed off the stage and slinked away. There was a back exit in the warehouse. I ran for it. Burst outside into the cold night and kept running.

I hid out for a few weeks. First getting back into the old booze habit and then kicking it again. When I got up the strength to go outdoors for the first time, it was like the whole thing never happened.

That's when I found out about Mike leaving for Guam.

"You'll never get me now!" he wrote in his last blog, almost as if he were writing to me directly. Confused, I stalked him relentlessly online until I found a recent picture of him shirtless by a bunch of crumbling homes on a dirt road.

That's when I knew things had come full circle. Mike was back in Guam fixing air conditioning units, and I had just bumped into some really great folks at the gas station who invited me to a Baha'i Faith temple, where I immediately joined up. There's this guy named Paul who started teaching me right away.

"Love one another!" he yelled at me, smacking me across the face. "Humble yourself before your maker!" he screamed, jumping up and down. "Be a joy to the sorrowful, a sea to the thirsty, a haven for the distressed, a gem on the crown of wisdom!"

ANGELICA

Johnson licked his lips, puckered them gently, and leaned forward. With his eyes closed, he pictured a breast—a single, gigantic, beautiful breast, backing enough explosive power to decimate a small country.

The breast in his mind, pink and soft, was replaced by a crater where Manhattan had once been. The crater jumped to Africa, then to Russia, then to the Middle East, settling someplace in Afghanistan with a plume of smoke rising up into the stratosphere and the entire continent rumbling.

The metal was cold and oddly bumpy against his lips. It was reminiscent of a moment from childhood, alone in a city park, leaning against the colorful metal pole holding up the rickety tube-shaped slide on the playground. Although, he couldn't remember if he had actually kissed the metal pole, or had merely thought about it. The sensation was strong and clear, but he could have simply *thought* about kissing it to know what it would feel like. Sure enough, it felt like *this*.

His eyes opened. A small spot of saliva glistened where his lips had connected, right on the exact tip of the warhead.

People often develop mental illness in their early twenties, Jackson remembered. Why is that? Is it the stress? Bad genes? A cursed adolescence coming to haunt you at the outset of adulthood?

Back home, it was hurricane season and all of Florida was supposed to get hit hard. A lot of the other guys in the service had wives or girlfriends back home—even kids. They had ambitions to earn degrees, get stable jobs, and settle into a vanilla suburban lifestyle with guilty beers and church on Sunday. In place of any of that, Jackson had Rita—that was her name this year—the hurricane. His whole life he'd loved nothing more than to watch her move in off the Atlantic. On the TV screen, he couldn't help sexualizing the nightmarishly serene hole in her middle.

One year, when he was fourteen, Bernadette demolished his foster home. She plowed straight through, thrashing around like a wild boar trying to break free from a cage, howling chaotically like a cartoon version of a pissed-off banshee. He abandoned his foster parents shortly after. As soon as he was old enough, he joined the army.

Mental illnesses are just like any other ailment. You can keep it a secret if you want to. The voices, the visions, and the overpowering obsessions—you don't have to say a thing. If it erupts, then let it erupt. But don't give it away. Don't give it a name. Don't, for God's sake, make it petty.

The warhead was a gigantic breast again when the sergeant entered.

"Jackson!"

"Yes sir!"

"Does that warhead have a home?"

"Uh…!"

"Does it have a family? Children? A horoscope or a favorite restaurant?"

"I don't know sir!"

"Well you should know! You should know every last biographical detail because she is your best friend. She is your mother, your sister, your mistress, and your wife. And tomorrow she will go down as the most important woman of this century."

"Yes sir!"

"Now, let's try this again."

"Yes sir!"

"What's her name?"

"It's, uh… Angelica sir!"

"And where is she from?"

"The U.S. of A. sir!"

"Good! Now, let's make sure the whole world knows it, Jackson."

"Yes sir!"

The sergeant handed Jackson a rolled-up decal.

"Brand her like a fat hog before the slaughter!" yelled the sergeant, saluting before he stomped off.

"Yes sir!"

Jackson licked his lips and unrolled the gigantic decal: a bright red, white, and blue American flag. Flailing his tongue left, right, up, and down, he spread his saliva all over the back of the decal until his mouth was gummy with the toxic adhesive. Light-headed, he smoothed the decal against the side of the warhead.

Mother, daughter, mistress, wife—the hurricane lay in wait for the morning air strike. "I am the hurricane now. I am the maker of destruction," said a voice in the back of his mind as he pulled himself into a secret chamber in the bowels of the hurricane's maniacal eye.

CALTRAIN NORMCORES

On Caltrain passing through Palo Alto on a Friday night. All these smart people with normcore on their foreheads. Unexpectedly, right around Stanford, the train stopped and locked everyone in. The normcores didn't say a word, though a guy named Scotty talking on the phone instantly hung up to dial his mom about the delay.

"All you normcores are trapped now!" said the train conductor over the intercom.

A few homeless people riding the train for warmth looked around with genuinely confused expressions, like, "What's a normcore?" The people who noticed this rolled their eyes and their foreheads flashed sarcastically, "Let me Google that for you."

Someone in the front car had already come up with an app to get the train started again. Not even a minute later, almost everyone on the train had downloaded the app and suddenly the train was moving at its usual pace. If you ever needed to open the doors, the app would do that, too.

There was some grumbling from the intercom. Then the conductor yelled, "Suck on this, normcores!" Then he explained how he put the train into top speed, manually locking it that way, and then rigged the tracks ahead to put the train on the wrong side for an inescapable collision.

"So, this should completely override the conductor's controls—even his manual lock of the top speed function," said a guy in brand new sneakers, talking to his neighbor.

"I think that's almost as good as mine," said the neighbor, adjusting his glasses as he scrutinized the code. "But I solved the problem just a little better here [pointing to code] by representing the train controls on a user's device in the shape of emojis, so even a kid with no language skills could override the evil conductor."

"That's really good... Darn it, I always forget about user experience!"

"Hey, your code has some good qualities, too. Let's take the best of yours and the best of mine together. Then we'll get a cool name and make a startup. No one will ever need to fear evil train conductors ever again."

"That's great! I'm in!" said the first guy. Standing up in his new sneakers, he directed his normcore forehead message throughout the train: "We have the perfect startup idea ready to launch! All we need is a few million in investor capital. Who wants to seed us the first six million to get us going?"

While a few investors looked over the proposal's ROI included in the attached cloud message, another person had just created a GPS app that could predict the time of the collision ahead. Sharing the information on normcore local, everyone paying attention started to panic. There was only about a minute left. Someone else had a new app estimating the time it would take to get the startup capital for the life-saving app to be on the market and ready for download: six months. A few people opened up the doors, using the app from earlier. They eyed the passing scenery with horror. They began frantically snapping pics of their last moments to upload to the cloud.

Along with a bunch of sentimental cloud-local pics, news began spreading throughout the train that the conductor had emerged from his cabin. But it wasn't good news. The evil conductor (he didn't have normcore on his forehead, people murmured with dread)—the evil conductor was grabbing people's mobile devices and smashing them!

To fight back, the people in the train's top deck started throwing their sneakers at the conductor, but that just seemed to make him stronger with rage.

"Code your way out of this!" he said, stomping up and down on a pile of mobile devices.

Scotty, the guy who had been on the phone with his mom, looked down at the pile of smashed devices with tears forming in his eyes.

He stood up, his kaki pants pulled up to his belly, his sneakers—overly worn, but still much loved—tied with perfect bows. His normcore on his forehead glowed neon red.

It was Friday night and he had a date with his mom. No way this evil conductor was just going to ruin everything.

Scotty reached over his head and pushed the little button on the top of his spine. The neon glow went dim, then vanished as his normcore software powered off.

Long ago, before the kaki pants, sneakers, baseball cap, and button-down shirt (untucked), Scotty had studied judo every Thursday night. His sensei, Steve, was the coolest guy he'd ever known.

"This is the move that will kill a man," said Steve. It was the last thing Steve ever taught Scotty, before his mom enrolled him in programming boot camp.

"This is the move that will kill a man," said Scotty, raising his voice for all of normcore to hear.

Ten seconds before the train wreck. Still six months before the startup funding deal would be made. Half of normcore on the train was about to jump.

"Hye-ya-wah-ka-cha!" Scotty yelled.

The evil conductor fell, crashing onto a mound of destroyed tech devices.

Five seconds before the terrible crash. Too late for the startup deal. The main donor just bailed, jumping out the train door right into a condo construction zone. At that moment, the train slowed. Just in time, it didn't switch over to the wrong track.

A few stops away, a middle-aged woman stood anxiously beside the Caltrain station. She held a shopping bag with a brand new pair of sneakers for her son—a present for all his hard work and good grades.

Her normcore received a message. "See you soon, mom!"

ONE HANG UP

Sitting in the sun watching the drownings. The sign by the water said DO NOT INTERFERE. Penalties of $500 per interference. I didn't have that kind of money. But I did have my eye on a girl.

In my generation, it's okay to talk about money problems. It's even okay to talk about junk food problems. But we still have this one hang up. Talking about the drownings always has some kind of fine attached.

I couldn't take my eyes off her if I tried. I did try, a little. But what could it matter? What's she going to do, wipe away a lifetime of strong feelings and not drown? Just because some creep on the shore is staring at her? Yeah, right.

The next moment—that was the last I'd ever see of her slender calf muscles. At one point, she must have been quite the runner. Possibly a sprinter or maybe she ran hurdles in school. (Her knees rose gracefully over the big waves, giving me last glances of her calves).

Our parents' generation cared a lot about authority figures. If someone with a good chin and the right-sized publicity team said "Get a job and go to bed on time!" it would be done. It wasn't okay to look shabby or skimp on your daily exercises. God save you if you stayed up past curfew eating cream puffs!

Know what I did today? Got up at noon and ate leftover pizza, licking the pepperoni grease off my fingers. Didn't get dressed till after 3:00. Drank cheap beer on the sidewalk with my buddy Mike, who came by just to brag how he stays up later and later each night. Not for any reason, just for fun. Something to live for. Now he's stayed up two days straight and he said if he falls asleep it's just because beer makes him nod off.

It was never supposed to be a competition, but now that I think about it, I guess it is. Who snubs authority figures best, him or me?

Then I woke up drunk at the beach. A few of the cans around me still had some booze in them. I finished them off while watching the drowners. Mike, I figured, was probably still wide awake somewhere. Guess he wins when it comes to staying up. Oh well.

Her cute ass was gone by now. I could have stared at it all day, but now it was gone. Her underwear was just the kind I like: minimal. In this case, white, no frills.

We don't like authority figures in my generation. We don't like rulers and rule makers. It's okay to drive fast and have sex in the park or at the bus stop. You can get any drug you want. You can worship any gods you want and yell how much you hate the government till you're blue in the face. If you ever see a cop, kick him in the nuts or go home, that's our generation's anthem. But we still have this one hang up. We can't say a word against the drownings without becoming slaves to rule makers, just like our parents. And that's bad. It's the worst thing. Also, there's the fine. On this beach, that's $500. Not cheap.

There she goes, I thought sadly. Water up to her lower back. Next big wave will be up to her shoulders. She'll be swept away. Bet she just had too much, that's all. What could have been her problem? Too many drugs? Too loud punk rock? Too much free time or an overload of sex?

Just then she turned and took a glance back at the shore. She caught me staring at her. Wow, those eyes! Hell yeah I stared back. A wave came up to her neck. She lifted up but the wave didn't carry her away. It pushed her slightly back to the shore.

She took a step out to sea again. I thought she'd make a dive. The next wave already building. But instead she looked back again. I raised my beer to her.

She smiled at me.

It was the first time I'd ever heard of someone smiling at a drowning. Generally it's a pretty somber, personal affair. But there she was. Smiling as the sharks circled. As the waves crashed over her head.

"That'll be five-hundred bucks, buddy."

It was Mike, standing over me with a fresh case of beer.

"Shut the hell up," I said.

"No, man. I saw you looking at the drowner like that. Caught you raising your beer up like a big stop sign. Sending those not-cool messages with your eyes. That's as good as a violation. And I should know. I'm a licensed Freedom Generation Enforcement Officer."

"Oh yeah? Since when did you become FGEO? You're the laziest piece of shit I've ever—"

"One of the things I did while staying up. Figured it would help me stay awake if I had something to do."

He was just handing me a ticket when I realized that the girl was gone. I jumped to my feet in a panic.

"Shit! Shit, man! She's gone!"

"She's what?" Mike asked, eyeing me suspiciously and already taking out another ticket. It's forbidden, of course, to express regret over a drowner, especially during the course of a drowning.

The idea of another fine was too much. From Mike, of all people. I ripped the pen out of his hand. I punched him in the face. Then in the gut. Then kicked him when he was down. I took both tickets and tore them to shreds. Yelling at the top of my lungs, I ran for the waves, right for the place where the girl had gone under. For the first time in my life, this felt like freedom.

SMALL TOWN DATE NIGHT

No way our town is ready for the future. We're already passed up, but get ready to be literally wiped out—I mean actually obliterated. When the future gets here.

At the Ravioli House with my new wife. God, she's got the best skin. You've never seen skin like this before. Sometimes I have to stop thinking just to touch it. Everything goes away when I focus in on how real it is.

"What are you thinking about, Ansel?"

"Huh?"

"I know you've got something going on up there."

"Oh yeah...yeah..."

I haven't told her about how screwed we are. Our town.

"How's your ravioli? It's not too soggy, is it?"

"No, it's fine," I confirm, taking an extra big bite, taking my time chewing. The restaurant was completely empty, as it tended to be at this hour—right when they open. I was in luck in this respect. So far, so good, I thought, glancing around the restaurant. I looked back at my wife with my healthiest, damn-that's-some-good-ravioli sort of smile.

How well do I know this woman? I asked myself, my grin fading. I had to look away from her face to process this thought. Her skin was too lovely. You can't critique a creature with skin like that, not when you're looking right at it. I found myself looking at my ravioli, with its oily, squishy surface. Yes, my critiques held. I didn't know this woman whatsoever.

The Ravioli House means date night, so afterwards we went out for a drink. We walked the streets. Our one main strip for downtown. Old cars parked on the street next to coin-operated meters. It's almost a shock not to see horse-drawn carriages.

When the future hits, this street will be the first to go.

My wife moved closer and caught hold of my swinging hand, capturing it like a balloon that might have floated away. Or maybe like a rickety old carriage that might otherwise have been pushed off a cliff. And good riddance to it. Her hand fit just right; even when I made no effort to hold it, I was holding it like holding something dear to my heart.

This felt like I was home—her hand in mine. When the street is destroyed, I decided, it won't matter so much if this hand is still here to hold.

"You've got that goofiest face tonight," my wife laughed, poking my cheek with her free hand.

"Hey!" I pulled my hand out of hers and patted my beard. "What's that even supposed to mean?"

"It's like the wrinkles on your forehead are trying to escape, like they're wiggling themselves loose to go on vacation."

I found myself staring into her eyes. The initial flash I sent her way was certainly a hard one. It was the look you may give to an enemy, of sorts. But a moment later, after getting into her eyes just a millimeter deep, my gaze softened.

The eyes are tough. Definitely a point of contention. They can go either way. Sometimes they're friendly and worth diving into; other times it's just the skin all over again—enchanting but untouchable.

At the bar, we found seats at a table in a dark corner. It's only been about a week since the wedding. The wedding? It's still called that, I believe? One week, anyway. And this only our second date night. The first time we went out, it was a Tuesday, so that hardly counts. This time it's Friday night. That doesn't mean much for our backwoods town, but it does mean more uncertainty. More unknowns—like people I don't know popping up and butting into my business.

"Well, look who it is," said John, the bartender. Overly friendly and one of the few people I let get away with it. "The town's best looking love birds!"

"We'll have a scotch neat, John."

"And the lady?" he asked with a smile as if it were a fantastic joke.

"She's fine," I said.

"She sure is!" he winked, walking away.

My wife was all smiles. "What a perfectly friendly guy! You don't mind how I winked back at him, do you? Because of course I didn't mean anything by it. And I certainly don't mean to upset you—the only man for my heart."

"Where did you pick up that phrase, only man for my heart?"

"Nowhere, I suppose. I put the words together myself, just for you."

I sat back in my chair, folded my arms across my chest, feeling, for some reason...not irritable—*agitated*, perhaps.

"Does God exist?" I shot at her.

She smiled with her cheeks puffed out, chin tucked down, as if she were disappointed in me. "...I'm searching for the best way to say this," she said, apparently holding back the urge to roll her eyes. "I'm guessing there's something you want to hear."

"Forget it. How about this. When will I die?"

She was still processing this (or pretending to) when John came around with my drink.

"Glad to see you're so happy, Ansel. Nothing like a woman to make a man complete."

I nodded while still looking at my wife. Not sure what had gotten into me, but I couldn't stop myself. "What's the biggest news story happening right now? One that hasn't reached the mass media yet."

"Terrorist attack on Istanbul's airport," she said. John stopped to listen. "Thirty people dead, at least—the bodies are still being counted. At least one hundred injured. Sure you want to hear this, dear? It's awfully grim for a date night topic."

"You're right," I said. "That one was just for John. Hey, isn't she great?"

John, however, couldn't speak. He'd fallen for the trap. I caught the look in his eye. He was transfixed by her satin, glowing skin. From his vantage, he could certainly even see into a bit of her cleavage. God save him. God save all of us in this damned town.

    I was drunk when I finally got it out of her when I would die. Of course I wouldn't! "Not with me by your side, silly," she said. I looked into her eyes, lost myself, knew her more deeply than ever, and realized my town had already been annihilated long, long ago.

TERRITORIAL PISSINGS

I learned black magic as a kid. I fell into it one day at church while flipping through the hymn book. The text held a secret just for me. That's what I felt.

It said, "When peace like a river, attendith my way / When sorrows like sea billows roll / Whatever my lot, thou has taught me to say / It is well my soul."

Or, in other words, "Sneak out to the cemetery tonight and piss on the most pompous-looking headstone, praising Satan."

I was eleven at the time. I figured I must be the most evil kid in the whole town. All these people had love their hearts and wore clean clothes. I wore hooded sweatshirts with stains and heard the voice of the devil in my hymn book.

This was in Montesano, Washington, a logging town of 3,000. Kurt Cobain lived there as a kid. Back then, he was the most satanic person around. I had his band teacher, Mr. Nelson. "He played drums and sat in back with his hair long and unkempt," Mr. Nelson would say. Also I had his history teacher, Mr. Winbeckler. "Every year I give a lesson on Eastern religions. It's from this same lesson that Kurt got the name for his band. Nirvana."

Skip ahead a few years and you've got Territorial Pissings on the airwaves. "When I was an alien, cultures weren't opinions ... Just because you're paranoid don't mean they're not after you."

I snuck out Sunday night and walked a mile down the logging road in darkness so intense it had to be evil. No moon that night but there were plenty of bats.

I was pretty sure from what I'd heard in church that if I did black magic then I'd be cursed by God. Just look at what happened to Kurt. He lived a childhood of poverty and loneliness; he dedicated his life to angry music to exorcise his demons; he was catapulted into fame he didn't even want and overnight became the biggest rock star in the world; he married Courtney Love who probably looked great naked and was also more than likely into Satan herself. And then he died on heroin and will live for eternity as a god-like legend and a cultural symbol of youth and rebellion. What a shitty life, huh? Who would ever want that?

It was in Sunday school, in fact, where I first invited Satan into my heart. Mr. Kramer, the teacher, said there can be no conversing with spirits. No magical spells. No playing with a Ouija board, not even as a joke. Or else God will smite you.

"Gotta find a way, a better way!" screamed Kurt in my mind.

That played full blast in my head until all the angels were too scared to get close to me. And that's when Satan came in.

The thing with the hymn book happened next. I knew what I had to do.

In the cemetery, surrounded by crumbling gravestones, I unzipped and pulled out my eleven-year-old virgin prick. It was a powerful, magical wand in the night. The only gleaming thing in the world. The cemetery shaking under my feet, the trees towing over me, the bats shrieking all around.

"Gotta find a way," I chanted as an incantation, "a better way to get away. Gotta find a way…"

And the stream of piss poured down hot and wet, soaking the dignified gravestone of some random dead guy who probably croaked in old age after a dull life trusting in angels. Then I zipped up and ran home chanting the first words that came to mind, "It is well my soul."

KILLER'S TRANCE

I can slip into a killer's trance at any time.

"Show me," said the command sergeant.

"Okay," I said, already slipping into it.

The prisoners of war avoided eye contact as I approached. In killer mode, everyday annoyances matter more than ever, and that brings clarity to the task of picking a victim.

An older-ish POW caught my attention. The guy had a bloody patch covering half his face. That irritated me. When I'm in killer mode, that's the last thing you want to do—make me irritated.

I snapped his neck in just the right way, killing him instantly.

"How's that?" I asked, switching back into human being mode.

"Not bad," said the command sergeant. "How did you learn that?"

"The killer's trance?"

"Yeah—whatever you just did there. One second you're just standing here looking complacent, the next—bam, you kill someone."

"I'm not too sure," I said. "I was probably just born with it. Anyway, it certainly wasn't basic training!"

We both laughed.

The command sergeant gave me an assignment. In preparation, I would daydream about how it would go.

At first I was excited and honored at the opportunity. But then I started to have doubts. This wasn't like me to have doubts. It came to the point where I would lay awake at night rationalizing my ability, explaining its value—all the while wondering if I actually held this power, or if I had just made it up.

People become killers all the time. It's a part of all of us! I'm just blessed with the ability to turn this mode on and off at a moment's notice (I explained to myself).

By the second day out on my mission, I had completely lost the ability. I had thought about it too much. And now it was gone.

"You okay?" asked the guy driving the jeep through the jungle.

He had been irritating me nonstop for the past twelve hours, but it seemed I couldn't do anything about it.

"Yeah, I'm just fine," I said. "Now shut the hell up and quit slowing down every two seconds."

"You want to drive?"

"No," I said, more irritated than ever.

I closed my eyes and tried for the millionth time that day to slip into the trance. I felt around for that door, that pathway, that window—whatever it was I needed to step into, or through. Nothing.

I was nervous, that was the problem. I couldn't focus.

"What is it that you do again?" the driver asked. "You have some kind of secret weapon, right?"

"I can slip into a killer's trance at any time," I said. I tried to make it sound like a threat.

Swatting at a mosquito for the tenth time, I missed again. Nothing to do but let the tiny monster suck me dry.

We came to a river. The driver helped me inflate a raft.

"You ever been this deep in the jungle?" he asked.

"Everything is my backyard," I said. "It's all the same to me."

He drove off. Now it was just me, this raft, this river, and about a hundred miles before I had to perform.

This deep in the jungle, you're surrounded by killers on all sides. If it's not a spider or a snake, it's a tiger, a hippopotamus, or a swarm of piranhas. You can't even think about touching the flowers or the berries—they'll all kill you.

Two days into my river journey, I had developed a true respect for the warlord enemy I was supposed to kill. If he lived in this place, he outsmarted death at every turn.

On the last stretch of my journey, I closed my eyes, dropped my paddle, and waited for the worst. I still couldn't figure out how to get into the trance. I had lost hope. I didn't care what happened next.

Flying through some rapids, I was thrown from the raft. My body crashed into sharp rocks. The piranhas immediately came for my blood. A river snake wrapped its body around my ankles and sunk its fangs into my gut. Just then I was pulled from the river by a tiger's jaws, chomping into my shoulder. A poisonous tree frog landed on my nose as my body was drug out of the river, along with the giant snake and a family of jumping piranhas.

Bleeding on all fronts with my legs turning blue, one arm grew numb as the other began to tear out of its socket. I used the last ounce of life in my numb arm to fend off an attack of black, biting spiders.

I can't say what happened after that. Whenever I slip into the killer's trance, I can't remember much. But I remember my head felt clear and the world felt right.

The next thing I knew, I was back at the army base. I was torn up, disfigured, and suffering from god knows how many types of poisons and infections in my blood stream. As the command sergeant pinned a gold metal on my breast, I tried to slip away again.

"Where are you going, private?"

"I'll show you."

SANTA CRUZ SEX CULT

Skirting along the California coast on Highway 1, drivers occasionally point a finger up to a seemingly random assortment of hills just north of Santa Cruz. "That's the place if you're looking to join a sex cult."

Santa Cruz is well known as a hub of freaks, so it's expected for local gossip to ring with a certain undertone of perversion, making sex cults the perfect topic of conversation.

"What do you mean by 'sex cult,' exactly?"

Many responses are given in answer to this question. More often than not, people who point to a random hill along the coast in California and say, "That's the place for sex cult meetings"—more often than not, such people really don't know what the hell they're talking about. They really just want to hear the sweet sound of their own voice saying words that will catch the attention of whomever happens to be within earshot.

Alternatively, it's like this: You're driving along the coast, looking around, gripping the wheel, turning with the turns, flying along like the best part of any high-stakes race—the victory lap. Over to one side is the ocean. Your heart soars in life-affirming awe. You take another swift turn and glance up to the sky. Inland, you see the lush tree-covered hills. For a moment, you truly feel at peace—satisfied and content, you swear, as you have never known possible. You are so overjoyed that you must somehow share your happiness. Looking up at the proud hills, you speak the first words that come to mind. "You see that hilltop up over there? That's the home of real life sex cult!"

People worry quite a lot about earthquakes and droughts. If the world itself isn't destroying itself, then the universe itself certainly is. The universe loves destruction and chaos. Until the day people find themselves somehow immortal, they *should* worry. What are we but sitting ducks, marked and numbered under death's microscope?

Also the costs of living keep rising and vacation time is increasingly difficult to come by. Once you actually find enough time and money to get out of your house and go someplace, you automatically either need to find a restroom or you want food. Just to put things in perspective (you clear your throat, making sure that everyone is listening), suddenly you raise your voice above the terrible screeching of tires and clapping of distant thunder, "So, I've heard that right up there is the place where some sort of sex cult holds its meetings."

The inevitable response comes right on queue. "What exactly do you mean—'sex cult'?"

"You know? I'm not really sure..." you answer, trying to sound as mysterious as possible.

RICHARD DAWKINS BY THE LIGHT OF THE FULL MOON

Seven witches gathered at London's Highgate Cemetery to cast a spell on Richard Dawkins. They were dressed in black with hoods and shawls, like superheroes in mourning. As the sun went down, they placed candles on top of nearby headstones, making long shadows dance and flicker on all sides.

"Fuck you, Richard Dawkins," they chanted quietly.

A special potion (wine with mugwort and other herbal additives) was passed around. One of the witches snuck away to pop open a fresh bottle of merlot while the chanting continued.

"Fuck you, Richard Dawkins."

"Okay, it's starting!" a witch named Ada exclaimed. She was holding a cellphone, which was streaming a live speech by Dawkins at Oxford University. The witches gathered around to watch.

"You are stupid, stupid people only fooling yourselves," said the esteemed atheist and evolutionary biologist, his voice projecting authoritatively from the phone's tiny speaker.

On the screen, the camera pulled back to show the audience: a group of Wiccans, palm readers, fortune tellers, Ouija board enthusiasts, followers of Cthulhu, believers in Odin, and other fanatics of the occult and the esoteric.

"There is nothing magic about the world, and there is certainly nothing truly magical about your spells, paranormal beliefs, prophesies, curses, and whatever else you have chosen to form your identities around."

"Curse his eyeballs, that they might pop right out of his face and go rolling around on the floor, where he'll step on them," said a witch named June, holding the spell-casting broomstick.

She passed the powerful item to the witch on her left, a runaway teenage girl named Sammy.

"Curse his head, so that his hair might catch fire and for that fire to form a mirror in his soul so he has to look at himself in the mirror for all eternity, not able to see anything else except for how mean and ugly he is."

Gina, a lifelong witch and equally dedicated punk rock girl, was suddenly caught between the wine bottle and the broomstick.

"Come back to me," she said, dead serious, taking the wine bottle and letting the broomstick be passed along to Karen.

"Curse his luck," said Karen, "so that everything he touches turns to shit, including his food."

With each curse cast, the girls became increasingly excited. Another bottle of wine was popped open. One of the witches lit a joint mixed with suma root and Avena sativa for stimulation of the libido. Another witch burned sage. As Dawkins' voice rose in anger and disgust, the witches began to undress and touch each other.

"To live successfully, we must engage with the world—with the world as it actually exists, not as we project it to exist based on unsubstantiated beliefs. If prayer worked, we would see the results of prayer. And yet there is absolutely zero evidence ever documented of prayer's effectiveness. If you have two sick children, you give one prayer and the other penicillin, guess which child gets well? The answer, of course, is obvious. The same is true for casting spells and playing around with magic. By engaging with these things, you are not engaged with what is real in the world, and so you undermine the core of human progress."

"Curse his soul," said Georgia, holding the broomstick like a microphone, "I hope he burns for all eternity in hell!"

Ada took the broomstick next, rubbing it between her legs as she cried, "Curse his big, fat, self-important brain, that it might explode in his head and his old, grey cortex might splatter all over the witches in the crowd, and so that they might eat his brains."

June crept behind Ada, kissing her neck and caressing her inner thighs as Ada made good use of the full broomstick handle.

"Go ahead," said Richard Dawkins, "cast a spell on me! Pray to your favorite god to have me expire in a puff of smoke! Sick the devil on me while you're at it!"

"Aww," moaned Karen, leaning against a headstone with Sammy's head sinking down between her open legs. "Fuck you, Richard Dawkins," she said between moans.

"Fuck you, Richard Dawkins," said Ada, kissing June and fondling her breasts.

Richard Dawkins loosened his tie and took off his jacket. "Is it getting hot in here?" he asked the crowd, taking a sip of water.

The camera zoomed out again, showing the entire auditorium turned into a giant orgy of spell-casting witches and occultists moaning in ecstasy.

"Fuck you, Richard Dawkins," they chanted, until Ada muted her phone and flung herself, body and soul, into an unholy tidal wave of multiple orgasms.

LAST DAY AS AN URBAN LEGEND

An urban legend sprang up about a guy who doesn't live paycheck to paycheck. I felt the animosity levels immediately rising in the streets. While walking into a coffee shop on 24th Street in San Francisco, a homeless man stepped into my face. "I don't like you," he said. I knew what he was talking about. I didn't have to ask.

"It's not me," I said in a hurry, hearing gunshots nearby. "I'm just getting coffee with the last few cents I have left." The people in the coffee shop probably heard me say this. I felt awkward as hell as I ordered my coffee. Handing the barista a ten-dollar bill for my three-dollar coffee, it was obvious I had stretched the truth.

At the next table over from me, a group of businessmen were discussing the situation. "How could it be done?" They wanted to know. One of them commented: "If you just make a decent amount of money and live below your means, it could be possible. Technically, there could be a fair percentage of the population that could pull it off." They grumbled and shifted in their seats. "Well, I just don't believe it," a middle-aged man stated irritably. He looked over and gave me a death-glare.

I was just about to leave the coffee shop when I realized that the barista hadn't given me back my change. The guy had simply pocketed my extra seven bucks. He must have sensed that I wasn't paying attention. How can anyone pay attention with those gunshots?!

Another one went off right outside. It was the third in the past half hour. A few police sirens were coming closer and closer.

"How about this guy?" one of the businessmen said in a hushed voice. "He just paid for a small coffee with a ten. And didn't get his change back...!"

I told myself these guys were on my side. Nothing kills fear better than a good lie. They saw it, too. The barista ripped me off. They knew. Moral support!

They were all looking at me.

When you want to appear casual, you can make yourself big by clearing your throat. I tried that. Then I gave a loud sniff. Look how confident I am! Not trying to hide...! I tried my coffee. It was too hot to touch. An inch from my lip, the steam burned.

Definitely couldn't leave yet. In these times it's almost criminal to leave a full cup of coffee.

"Didn't you forget something?" One of the businessmen asked suddenly. He was calling me out. I had no choice. I had to engage.

"What?"

"Your change. You paid with a ten."

Okay. I would get a to-go cup. That would solve everything. There's no problem. Everything is cool. I acted surprised. My eyebrows narrowed. I thought about it.

There was nothing to do but get it over with. I got up to ask. The barista gave me a dumb look.

"Yeah?"

"I didn't get my change back, I just realized…"

"What do you mean?"

"I think I gave you a ten. For the coffee. I could be wrong. Never mind. Forget it."

Back at my seat. I couldn't handle this tension. The barista's rising level of irritation in his face. I had to leave no matter what. Coffee still too hot…

Just as I was standing to leave, a cop entered; his gun was drawn. It was too late to turn back. I marched toward the door. For some reason I was still holding my coffee. I had to look casual. I took a sip, burning my tongue.

To my horror, one of the businessmen suddenly shouted:

"It's him! Stop him!"

Still heading for the exit, I looked around, as if wondering who the guy was talking about. At the same time, the bum entered, immediately holding up his fists as if ready for a standoff.

"Everybody calm down!" yelled the cop, pointing his gun in all directions.

Seizing the moment, I splashed my coffee into the face of the bum, scalding him and pushing him aside as I made a run for the door.

"Hey!" yelled the cop. "Stop! Put your hands up!"

I glanced over my shoulder to see the cop collide with the wailing bum. They both crashed to the floor and began to brawl. Bursting into the street, I sprinted across 24th and headed down Bryant Street towards Cesar Chavez.

Horrified by every set of eyes I encountered, I ran more furiously than ever. By the time I reached the summit of Bernal Heights, I was absolutely beat. Leaning over, hands on knees, I raised my head just long enough to catch an eyefull of the San Francisco skyline, the Bay, and Oakland off in the distance. I heard one last gunshot. Then silence.

BONA FIDE FORMALDEHYDE

I straightened my tie and threw my shoulders back, thinking: "So this is it. Where they take you when you first start a business." My company was counting on me. Two employees, one intern, and… No, that's everybody. And myself. Good people. Excellent workers.

"I came here kicking and screaming!" I reminded myself. But shook fifty people's hands in the lobby and made my easy-going smile over and over.

There were a few of the big boys and then a lot of us little guys at the licensing convention. One guy I shook hands with, his nametag said "Earl."

"Good to meetcha, Earl!" I said.

"And good to meet you…Bona Fide Formaldehyde?"

"Oh—ha, ha! Yeah, I thought the tag was for company name. Pretty stupid! I'm Bart."

We shook hands again.

I asked him: "You think we're gonna leave here, you know, wiping the Kool-Aid from the corners of our mouths?"

"I'm not sure I know what you mean," said Earl in a guarded tone, a little suspicious.

Uh-oh!

"You're just one of the little guys…right?" I nudged him, suspicious myself. "Like me?"

"New to business, yeah."

"Okay, me too. I'm just paranoid, that's all. Afraid we'll walk out of here with stains all down our shirts and the Kool-Aid still dripping off our chins."

Just then the extremely pleasant background music turned off. It was like the door had been locked behind us. Had it? It was like: now you're trapped.

A voice said over the intercom: "Please take your seats. The keynote address will begin in five minutes."

"So you sell formaldehyde?" asked Earl as we made our way into the main conference room.

"Yep. Make it, sell it, market it, live it, breath it! How about you? Want a sample?"

I took out a little packet of liquid pure formaldehyde and gave it to him.

"Thanks."

"Any time, pal! How about you? What's your enterprise?"

"I just opened a small massage parlor. I'm a masseur."

"Oh, good for you, Earl!" I said, holding back a laugh.

A *masseur*!!!

It was like a cattle call. All of us cattle scrambling for seats. I forgot about Earl as I followed right on the tail of the best looking "little guy" tail I'd ever seen in a skirt. It was a black skirt tight-forming no matter how her ass moved and it was a wonder she hadn't been in business longer, whatever she was selling.

"Great view," I said to her, sitting down, "of the stage."

She gave that kind of polite fraction of a smile people give.

"Let me guess," I said, scratching my chin. "High-end clientele accounting services?"

That should flatter her, I thought! Or should I have said rocket science engineer? Little guys these days, they like the boring, brainy stuff.

She just smiled again. Same damn smile.

"My friend Earl here is a masseur," I said, condescendingly (couldn't be helped), pointing to my right. "Hey... Where'd he go?"

Oh, there he was. Three rows up. He'd abandoned me!

There is no loyalty among the little guys, I noted. I kept shoulders square. It's a battle ground around here. Can't show your vulnerabilities for a second.

"Claire" (per name tag) was reading the day's agenda. I leaned over to follow along.

- Keynote: Responsibilities as a Business Owner
- Regulations, Laws, and Licenses (small group)
- The New Ethical Business Culture (panel discussion)
- Always Closing vs. Always Building Relationships
- Lunch Break

"Excuse me," said Claire. "Are you looking down my blouse?"

"God no! I was looking at the schedule."

"Don't you have your own?"

She stood up. I played confused. Looked around.

"You're sitting on it," she said, moving away. I watched her make her way up a few rows and take the next empty seat—of course right next to Earl.

The keynote was about to begin. Everyone gradually shut up. I started sweating. A guy tested the mic behind the podium. One of the big boys. You can spot them from a mile off.

"I'd like to welcome our keynote speaker: founder of Mo Sales and author of *Awaken Your Corporate Giant*, Mitch Pilebaum!"

Cheers from all sides! Everyone loves them some Kool-Aid drinkers! Clap, clap, clap! Woo-hoo!

It was time for the ear plugs. Luckily I brought a pair of super silencers. Little guys all around me were already getting lulled into it. Carried off with the corporate mumbo jump. Their souls seeping away.

The guy on the stage, Mitch, was your typical macho-man sales hero. Just a flick of the pen to change the Earth from globe to cube. Wipes his shoes on God's face. Just like a doormat. Probably lives in fucking Malibu.

I must have drifted off. Next thing I knew, people were up and out of there seats. Walking away through all exits. What'd I miss? Was everybody already brainwashed that easily? Was I the only one with a soul left in this place?

I caught sight of Earl making his way towards one of the exits. The place was dead silent. Horribly silent like you're watching a move in the middle of a scene with the sound off.

I followed after Earl. The rotten girl Claire was also going towards the same exit. Hurrying after her, I caught a glimpse of her profile—just as lifeless and blank as everyone else's.

"I'll never be one of them!" I yelled inside my head. "I'll go into business and sell the best damn formaldehyde and never give in to corporate bullshit! I'll hold onto my ideals as if all the formaldehyde sales in the world depended on it!"

Herded into a small room. Earl and everyone started taking their shoes off and lying down on the floor. I didn't like the looks of this. "It's just a stupid workshop..." I reminded myself. Or was it?

Without thinking, I grabbed Earl by the arm right as he was about to lay down. "Earl," I said, "I've got to use the bathroom." My voice sounded weird. Oh, it was the ear plugs. I took them out. Early stood there watching like an idiot. "Come with me," I said again and gave him a wink.

He started to protest but I dragged him along. Claire gave us a sidelong glance. Some kind of grudge. Never trust people like her, whether or not they happen be rocket engineers.

In the bathroom. "Alright, Earl," I said, "please tell me you're still yourself."

"I thought you needed to..." he gestured towards the urinals.

"Never mind! Earl, listen up, what did they say in the big conference room?"

"Weren't you there?"

"Of course I was! But I took measures to protect against becoming a corporate zombie."

"Look," said Earl, shaking his head and backing away, "everything is fine, okay? Just come into the next room, take your shoes off and play along. This is the easy part. But it's important we don't miss it for the licensing exam..." He smiled like a real dope and then bolted for the door.

"Earl!" I hissed. But he was gone.

All was lost for poor, dumb Earl. I stood there in shock. But then I started to panic. How would I ever make it through? I couldn't hold out much longer...

Sweating, rubbing my face, I paced back and forth.

Just then someone entered. It was the big shot who gave the keynote—Mitch. One glance at him and immediately I booked it for the stalls. Jumped into one and slid the lock into place. Stood there. Waited for him to pee, get it over with, and leave. Then I'd figure out what to do next.

But he never unzipped. Never even made it to the urinal. He was at the sink. What was he doing, staring into the mirror like a creep? Then he turned on the water. Washing his hands...? Brushing his teeth! Clear sounds of teeth brushing. I leaned against the stall, furious.

A minute passed. Then two, then three. And he was still brushing away.

This cold sweat of mine transitioned into a burning-under-the-collar sweat. I was like a furnace. Sweat dripping down my back, dripping off my forehead onto the tile.

"What must he think I'm doing in here?" I wondered. That's what worried me the most.

Swish, swish, swish went his toothbrush.

A nervous tick of mine: I started toying with one of the formaldehyde packets I had with me. I tore it open. Gave it a good sniff.

There. I felt a little better. "See!" I yelled silently to myself. "You don't need any goddamn regulations! It's just formaldehyde and it's used in a million products—the magical ingredient!"

I squeezed it all out onto my hand. Slimy liquid goodness. Product of the century. Right here in my palm. Need to make some inexpensive flooring? This is the stuff for you! Need to embalm someone? Here you go!

Running my hand through my hair, I discovered a whole new use. Hair gel!

I grabbed another packet from my pocket. I grabbed a handful of them. Tore them open all at once and breathed in that glorious scent certain to make of me a rich man. Sniffed so hard my nose bled. Licked my fingers, rubbed my hands all over my face.

"Regulate this, you idiots!" I yelled. My voice echoed off the bathroom walls, but what did I care? Nothing. "Regulate this!" I kept on screaming.

More packets! Opening all of them. You take it all and you become invincible. That's the secret and that's why they want to regulate. To keep us the little guys.

Heaving, sobbing, high as a fucking gorilla on a spaceship, I remembered the keynote speaker brushing his teeth. I'd kill him!

Bursting out of the toilet stall, I staggered forward and looked around with bleeding eyes.

"Regulate this! I'd like to see you try!" I screamed at him, wherever he was. I kicked at the first definite shape I saw. But it was just a urinal.

I lost balance for a moment, my foot twisted. But I jumped about face and lunged toward the direction where the sinks had to be. Slipped and crashed onto the tile. That really made me go mad.

I slipped around on the floor for a few minutes looking for the exit when suddenly I heard footsteps. The door to the bathroom swung open and someone came in. A couple of guys. They grabbed me by the arms. Yanked me up. I put up a struggle, calling them out on their corporate mind control as they dragged me away.

"You can't regulate me!" I yelled, thinking now of my faithful employees, both of them, and my intern. There were people standing all around. All the newly brainwashed little guys. Earl probably looking as downtrodden as ever with his masseur paws hovering over Claire's stiff neck. Both of them envious of my moment of glory.

"You can't regulate me! I am Bona Fide Formaldehyde! A naturally occurring organic compound! I'll sell you a taste right now on discount. Come and get some. Free sample!"

E-THERAPY GIRLS

I felt like I couldn't trust my e-therapist. I realized this right after I shared with her my war history. The fact is, I made that all up. The people I killed, the officers I disappointed, the way I escaped and hid for years alone in Afghanistan. I never went to war or even joined the army. That's not my problem. I'm afraid of people not liking me. When I talk to my e-therapist I can tell her everything—just not that.

Thinking this over, pacing around the room, I'd lost track of time. Shit, I was late. So much for collecting my thoughts. I was suddenly more upset than ever. Deep breath, deep breath, I thought, clicking the connect button; she was already online.

"Hi, Barry," she said, beating me to the hello.
"Hey, Erica. Heh. Good to—"
"How are you today?"
"Good."
"That's great! So, let's—"

"How are you?"

"Oh? Oh, I'm good, too."

"Sorry."

"No, don't be sorry." She was strict with me like that. I kind of liked it. But then again, I wasn't sure.

She was smiling at me super encouragingly. She could make just about anyone feel encouraged. I smiled back.

"So," she said, "don't be concerned, but you're going to get a knock at your door anytime now."

"What do you mean?"

"Oh, nothing. Just thought I'd give you a heads up. You are at home, right?"

"You know where I live?"

"It's okay! There's really nothing to worry about. Last time we talked, you were telling me about your war adventures."

"I don't want to talk about that anymore."

"That's okay, Barry. But sometimes it's good to let it all out. Not hold anything back. When you hold things back, it doesn't feel good. Does it, Barry?"

"No."

"It's called repression."

"I don't even know who you are."

"Ha, ha! What do you mean? It's me, Erica."

"I've told you all about my family I ran away from as a kid, all about dropping out of college and living on the street, all about selling drugs and prostituting myself, all about my war history and all that. You haven't told my anything."

"You know, your history involves a lot of running away."

I sat there silently. E-therapy was a stupid idea. I just wanted someone to talk to at night—someone of more quality and substance than you find on all those dating sites. But it was stupid; I saw that now.

Erica was usually so great. But lately she had changed. She started looking at me funny. And I get nervous when people look at me like that. It was like she cared about me—like the way my last girlfriend looked at me right before I broke it off. When people give me that look, I start to pull away. Can't help it.

"What's that sound?"

"What sound?"

"Is someone at your door? I thought I heard—"

"I didn't hear anything."

"Oh. Well, okay. False alarm, I guess."

"What do you mean someone is coming to my door?"

"Hey, I'm supposed to be the one asking questions here, buddy."

"I think I've got to go."

"No, Barry. I'm sorry. Our session's just started…"

I was in a panic. That's the thing. My anxiety. It goes crazy. I never even knew I had anxiety so bad until I started e-therapy. Now it's all I ever think about.

"I've got to go," I said again. "I don't have to explain myself!"

I turned off the session. Listened for a moment. Then ran to the window. Outside, it was sunny and the street was deserted. But that didn't mean there couldn't be a sniper.

I was thinking crazy. No one wanted to kill me. More likely they were coming to arrest me. Erica had reported my war crimes. That was it.

I ran back to my computer. Logged into my latest dating site and looked up Paula. She'd know what to do even if she only wanted to be friends. She'd never said that to me, but I could tell. I know why. I got needy too fast. I needed her all the time. If she wasn't online right when she'd say she'd be, I'd get furious.

Of course she wasn't online.

I started writing her a note explaining everything. It was pointless. She only used my notes against me—especially when I needed help. I scrolled through all my other best prospects. Debby,

Anne, Sabrina, Kate, Shawna. There were about 50 of them. I really needed a pretty girl in this time of crisis. Someone who could really listen. But wouldn't you know: all the pretty girls were gone. What happened?!

It was time for action. I ran to my room and started packing.

So Erica wants to see me homeless? Fine, I'll be homeless. She wants me to run away from everything? I'll run! Will I join the army and kill people and run away from there, too? Sure! Why not! It's clearly the only thing I'm good at.

My room was suddenly torn apart. But I had my suitcase ready.

"Let's do this," I said out loud to myself. And it was the most exhilarating moment of my life. I was finally taking control. Running from the law! Scared of nothing!

I dragged my suitcase to the living room and peaked out the window.

Shit.

Too late. There were cars parked on either side of the street. Hadn't been there before. They were nondescript with tinted windows. Shit.

Panicking, seriously losing my cool, I ran back to open up my e-therapy session. I still technically had about ten minutes left. Maybe Erica would still be there.

No luck. She was offline. Screw this. I'd sue!

It was way too quiet in my apartment—and outside. I could sense something about to happen. Then I realized all the lights were on. You freaking idiot! I ran around flipping light switches off in every room. Then I sat in silence in the dark. Still no Erica online. I didn't have another appointment with her until next week. What was I supposed to do, wait here a week to ask her what the hell is going on—when any moment they might come and arrested me? I had to clear this thing up!

My last hope was to give in to my ultimate weakness. The girls of StripperCamBabes.

Logging on, the screen lit up with endless icons of hot babe profiles. Scroll over an image to get a sneak peak. Okay, I needed someone nice. A girl who could help me. In a very real, non-fantasy sort of way. Help me to overcome my fears, my dependence, my insecurities, my looming depression, my self-loathing, my sleeping problems, my commitment issues...

No one looked right. Too big, too small. That sort of thing.

Then my eyes did a double take. Wait a minute, huh?

I scrolled over, looked for a sec, clicked. The screen opened to the girl's profile page. Wow1CutieGirl was her name.

On this site, you had to pay to talk. My credit card was activated and I still had some credits pre-paid. I clicked the icon to go into live mode.

"Hey, Wow One Cutie Girl," I said.

She was laying there on a bed, leaning forward, legs curled under her. Wearing only lacy panties and a tight, baby blue tank top. No bra. Her breasts looked stellar. Her hair was pulled back. She wore glasses.

"Hey Tiger Wants Some," she responded playfully. My screen name sounded great, the way she said it like that.

"Hey," I said. I had never stuttered so little in my life. "Can you see me on your screen?"

"Only your profile picture."

"That's a cartoon. Can't you click something so you can actually see me? I can sure as hell see you."

"I get nervous when I see the person I'm talking to."

"Well I want you to look at me." I was really asserting myself. It felt great.

"Okay, one second," she said. And then: "Oh!" She paused, sort of repositioned how she was seated. Whatever she changed, her breasts sunk noticeably into her chest. "It's you," she said.

"Yeah," I said. I turned on the lamp next to my computer so she could see me even better.

"Yeah, it's me. And I've still got at least twenty minutes left on my e-therapy session."

"But you walked away," said Erica. "You ended it."

"Only to go pack my things."

"Pack?"

"Yeah, I'm leaving. I'm out of here."

"I don't understand. I really tried to help!"

"Well," I said, sitting back in my chair. "Maybe you can help me now."

She turned a little pale, then flushed. She caught the hint. I couldn't wait to hear what she said next. But she just sat there quietly, pulling into herself. She looked great.

Just then the doorbell rang. I froze.

"I think I heard—"

"Shut up!" I hissed, not in a mean way—scared.

"Just answer the door! It'll be okay!"

"Why, so they can arrest me?!"

"No one's going to arrest you! I know you're paranoid, but—"

"Oh, that's a great technique for a therapist."

The doorbell rang again. It was followed by a loud knock.

"Tell me who's there," I demanded.

"No," said Erica, even more worked up than I was. "It's a surprise!"

"Some damn surprise!"

"You have to hurry!"

"I will—when I jump out this window and run for the nearest train station!"

Just then my time expired—I was kicked out of exclusive live show mode. Immediately a few other guys' names popped up on the side of the screen. They came right out with copious varieties of lewd bullshit. I read all their messages. I couldn't help myself.

"Babe ur of age right? U look 14 w them small ass titties."

"Money on them tits is fo real. R they grl?"

"Dayum chicka it too hot in here for that tank. Take that shiz off!"

"I'll show you mine 4 free. Ok u ready?"

"Fine," I typed into the feed. "Have it your way. Just know I never killed anyone. I didn't quite college. I've never lived on the street and I never joined the army. I'm an engineer at a standout firm and I just happen to work from home a lot. Also e-therapy was the best part of my life until about 5 seconds ago."

In a blind rage, I marched to the door just hoping they'd tackle me, drag me away, and get it all over with quick. So much the better if they just started shooting.

"What?!" I yelled, yanking the door open.

Standing there right on my welcome mat was about the last thing I expected. A pizza delivery guy.

"Hey man, uh..."

"Yeah?"

"Pizza—mushrooms, olives, tomatoes—right?"

"I didn't order a pizza."

"Yeah, uh. It came with like special instructions. Already paid for. I'm supposed to say: 'Happy birthday to a true war hero.'"

I took the pizza. Slowly turned and closed the door. God. I'm not good with presents. Receiving anything just goes to prove I'm inadequate. But the thing did smell good. One has to eat. People who waste stuff—even presents—are scum. I can only sink so low. If this was a pizza, I'd eat it. So, standing in the dark in my kitchen, I had a slice.

Contemplatively on my third slice, I walked back to my computer. Figured it was time to get a new e-therapist. Start fresh.

Instead, I found a familiar face on the e-therapy site. Erica was there waiting for me. Fully clothed, wearing her professional black blazer without a hint of cleavage. Same glasses.

"I got the pizza," I said.

"I told you not to worry."

"So did you help get some guys off or what?"

"Maybe we both learned something today."

"I could tell you more war stories if that'll make you feel better."

"I would like that. Then I could help you get over your fear of people not liking you."

"How do you know about that?"

"It's pretty obvious."

"You're good."

"Thanks."

I shrugged, licked my fingers, and then carried on where I'd left off. Hiding out someplace in Afghanistan. Alone in a hovel, suffering from a bad case of shellshock and other mysterious ailments.

MUSTARD SLEEVE

Burger-joint bright yellow mustard surprised me on my sleeve. I felt blinded as I licked it off. I put on sunglasses and kept licking. Adding ketchup, salt, and a slice of pickle, I was no longer sure what I was looking at through my rock-and-roll lenses.

I took my shirt off because this had to be a tropical beach vacation, even though I swear I had just gotten off work on a dark evening and come to escape the cold in this burger joint without ever leaving town. But then I'd lost the mustard sleeve. The shirt was inside out. Where could that sleeve have possibly gone? Wasn't I just licking it? Then my sunglasses fell off. God, things became awkward real fast.

Panicking like the first and last time I ever tried romance over a cheap meal, I grabbed my uneaten half of a hamburger and the sticky bottle of mustard and ran outside into a homeless person, tripping head over heels shirtless, launching the mustard bottle into traffic, forever staining sunshine on someone's windshield like the dazzling yellow taste on my lips.

SUPERHERO VINCHENZO

Vinchenzo discovered marijuana one shitty day in February while skipping math class. Struck by hunger pangs like he'd never imagined, he fled school premises, determined that nothing would ever again hold him back from his dreams. Till abruptly, at the edge of a crosswalk, he halted. Across the street: Oscar's Burritos. "Oh God, burritos," Vinchenzo murmured longingly. The crosswalk sign said walk twice. Three times. Walk. Don't walk. Walk. At last his feet budged. The sign was saying don't do it, but he did anyway.

If only he had paid better attention in his math class, he would have known that his coins would never add up to the price of a burrito. First he counted 83 cents. Then he counted 76 cents. He felt the money growing smaller in his hand every second. If the line didn't move more quickly, soon he would be completely broke.

The cashier woman glared at him but he would not be intimidated. At that exact moment, he discovered the power of thinking on his feet. "Um, can I get some chips and salsa?" he asked. It was 50 cents. He ordered just in time with only four extra cents to spare.

With hunger pangs temporarily satisfied, he flew back to school, raising his arms like a champion as he raced through the crosswalk. Back at school, he felt in his back pocket just to be sure. Yes. The marijuana was still back there. Now he would only need to find a lighter and some paper so he could smoke it.

HOLOGRAM FREE ZONE

1.

Hologram Tupac attracted a crowd outside West Oakland Middle School. A bunch of sixth graders with joints on their lips stood before him in a row. They were the toughest kids in school. They skipped class to smoke joints whenever they damn well pleased.

"You here for the assembly?" asked Ross, the kid who always asked dumb questions.

"He can't talk, you idiot!" said Matt, the youngest dude on the FBI's watch list.

"Everybody's at war with different things," said Tupac. "I'm at war with my own heart sometimes."

Matt didn't like that. He went right up to Tupac and took a swing.

2.

Hologram Gandhi was taking a stroll around Lake Merritt. Two joggers slowed down, eyed him suspiciously, and kept running. Turning about-face, Gandhi joined them on their run.

"First they ignore you," he said, "then they laugh at you, then they fight you, then you win."

3.

Hologram Marilyn Monroe stood outside a liquor store in East Oakland. Every few minutes, some sketchy guy would come up behind her, lunge to grab her around the neck—grabbing nothing, he'd tumble onto his face.

"Sex is a part of nature," said Marilyn. "I go along with nature."

4.

Oakland fights gentrification with drug dealers and pick pockets. Oakland shoots up on your doorstep while making sculptures with the cat food leftovers even your rats are too prissy to touch. In a homeless man's musty stench, Oakland reminds you that history doesn't come easy and it never washes off. When punk bands unite to stop traffic outside your office, that's Oakland reminding you what really matters, though you'll probably never figure it out. When the the Hayward Fault brings the ceiling down as you're sleeping, that's Oakland telling you to get the hell out and go back to Pasadena, or whatever lame-ass city you came from.

5.

Community organizers got stoned, drunk, and made distortion ambiance with second-hand guitars while discussing the hologram crisis. Who's projecting holograms of dead celebrities all over our radical city?

"Our city is not the stomping ground of the establishment's idols!" cried one member, coughing furiously on his ganja.

"No!" cried another member, raising her fist. "We don't stand for celebrities! They're only the symbols through which the masses are disempowered!"

Together they began a chant—a secret chant to summon the Spirit of Oakland out from the tree roots, the gutters, the punk basements. They chanted all night until the air grew mysteriously chilled and musty—signs that the spirit had entered.

They opened their eyes and there in the haze of ganja smoke stood Jack London.

6.

With Jack, the community organizers marched through the streets. They marched around West Oakland Middle School, around Lake Merritt, and through the most perilous streets of East Oakland. No sign of the holograms.

As they walked, they spray painted on streets, sidewalks, houses, corner stores, and cars: "HOLOGRAM FREE ZONE."

"Life is not always a matter of holding good cards," said Jack London, "but sometimes, playing a poor hand well."

The community organizers held a long moment of silence each time Jack spoke. They shivered and glowed in the presence of his true wisdom.

Heading downtown, the organizers passed out their three most popular pamphlets:

> 1) "Busted Car Windows Make Us Beautiful!"
> 2) "Love Is a Gender Neutral, Multi-Racial, Long Haired, Non-Religious, Oakland Native!"
> 3) "There Are No Crime Statistics in Oakland, There Is Only THE STRUGGLE!"

7.

"There!" said one to the community organizers, pointing at the Tribune Tower. Everyone turned to see Hologram Gandhi climbing up the side of the building.

Meanwhile, a crowd had gathered outside the Fox Theater where Marilyn Monroe was floating into the sky. About fifty people were underneath her, mesmerized as they stared up her skirt.

"Quick, grab their wallets!" said Matt, and all his buddies began reaching into the back pockets of the distracted people in the crowd.

"Ross! What the hell are you doing?!" Matt hissed.

"Trying to take a picture up her skirt," said Ross.

"Idiot!" said Matt. "We're here to steal wallets. She's just the distraction!" he punched Ross in the gut to make him learn. "Get your shit together, man!"

Meanwhile, Tupac was doing a handstand on top of Oakland City Hall.

"Shows all week in a city near you!" said Tupac.

"Tonight in San Francisco, tomorrow in LA!" said Marilyn.

"Get your tickets now!" said Gandhi.

The three holograms floated up into a helicopter hovering overhead.

"You can't wait for inspiration," said Jack London to the organizers. "You have to go after it with a club." Then he flew into the sky, disappearing with the helicopter as it headed off towards San Francisco Bay.

"What?" said several voiced in the crowd. "They're not playing any shows in Oakland?"

"First the Spirit of Oakland leaves us..." one of the community organizers groaned, "and now my wallet's gone!"

TUSKS OF VARAHA

Dining alone in an Indian restaurant in London, ceremoniously consuming a steamy plate of curry mush, Harvey began sweating and picked up his napkin from off his lap, touching it to his forehead like petting a sacred good-luck moment of human dignity and sacred intuition.

Just then he conceived a dare for himself.

The proper way to put it looked cross-eyed back at him and winked. There it sat: the comic adjudicator from hell—the devil—with its fat gut and perfect whiskers and horns. Superintending pointless dares in Indian restaurants everywhere. Stewing after the pointless fallout. Utterly hysterical for more to come, for eternity.

Harvey deliberated. He was just drunk enough on beer to give a wink back. He did so and then emptied the remainder of his drink with a gulp.

"I dare myself to get a girl tonight. Or else go abstinent for a good solid pig's lifetime."

He grinned at his devil friend, the obese swine statue mounted upon a decorative table. Almost too much for all the clutter of the restaurant. Where hundreds of thousands of designs, pictures, and shapes dwelt enshrined in so many tapestries, trinkets, and figures.

"Monsieur," Harvey called to the waiter appearing with a water pitcher. "Exactly how long do pigs live on average, would you say?"

"I'm sorry. What is your question?"

"The average lifespan of a pig. What is it?"

The man followed Harvey's gesture toward the portly statue.

"I may not be understanding... That is Varaha, the boar. In Hindu, an avatar of the supreme god Vishnu."

"Perfect!" cried Harvey, scoffing. "There's my dignity. On the platter of a pig god."

"Yes, sir. Varaha battled the demon Hiranyaksha who had taken the whole earth into the cosmic ocean. The battle lasted a thousand years. Varaha defeated Hiranyaksha and carried the earth away in victory between his mighty tusks."

"Ah. And what are Varaha's powers?"

The waiter thought a moment.

"Varaha is the symbol of the earth returning again. It is the story of a new cosmic cycle."

Directing an ambiguous scowl at the pig, Harvey fell silent.

"More water, sir?" asked the waiter, clinking some ice cubes.

ORION'S TOOTH

Stargazing is a real thing I try to explain to my fellow creatures every chance I get. At the moment I have something stuck in my tooth, which doesn't sound like a very big problem until I explain that it's a dentist's probing instrument and along with it he has both of his entire hands shoved into my mouth. I can't speak and pretty soon my whole jaw is going to come ripping off my head when all I want to do is patch up a simple cavity.

In other circumstances, as I was saying, I would right this very moment be telling all about the marvels of stargazing. The last time I talked to a spry old Jack Russell Terrier about it, I started getting through to her right away. She hugged my knee and barked as I pattered her head. The way her playful nub of a tail wagged, I knew she understood completely.

    Dear lord, my jaw! Not to mention my aching tooth! And my dying face! I wanted to scream… The pain was almost intolerable. Why wasn't it numb yet? Numb thoughts, numb thoughts. Please dear god make it get numb already!

    This is exactly why I never go to the eye doctor, why I never get my hair cut, and why I only eat food that never requires the use of silverware. All of these things are impure and simply serve as distractions from stargazing. It was only when my tooth started to clearly rot itself out of my head that I knew I needed some professional help.

    This dentist may be the only one of my fellow creatures I ever refrain from telling about the wonders of stargazing. He may never get to know those incalculable joys. As I was saying, if I ever get out of here alive, I know exactly what I'm going to do. First thing, I'm going to head straight for the dog pound, then to the candy store, and then back into the hills for good.

PASTY

    I should not have told them espionage, thought Dukeman on the run, clutching his briefcase, out of breath after twenty steps. They interrogate me over a pasty. Asking why can't I pay in smaller change. Maybe because I am a classy international playboy. In what way, they ask?

Espionage, of course. That was my mistake. Should have said fashion. Or opera. Too many patriots to take a threatening joke from a foreigner. I just wanted that pasty.

"Stop him!"

"Stop him!"

"Stop him!"

"Stop him!"

That particular beef and potatoes one. Looking so crispy and bulging. The dimple of hot brown insides oozing. Would like to tongue right inside it on a park bench someplace where we would not be bothered. Not by English bastards or anybody—French, Germans, Spanish: I don't like none. And why not. While this yelling hounds after. That's him! Menace to the queen! Spy! Thief! Creep!

"Huh?"

"What?"

"Who?"

"Me?"

I don't know anything about this. I'm just out for a jog. Cheers. Top of the— Ahhh.

Dukeman tripped over some hundred-year-old cobblestones. Didn't fall but there went the briefcase flying. Crashing open—contents aspew. And so instead of feeding pasty crumbs to thankful pigeons, I'm bending over to peck at my scattered capital—

—Adding to the meaninglessness. Because that is what in fact accrues. On days when you—admit it—accept losses the same as gains. Mesh both into focus. Finally to see yourself the heir to everything. Now trying to explain this encompassing apathy. When what I have is the expanse of my sover'n self, and all I want is a focking pasty.

NATIONALIST SWEETHEART

I had every right to be a nationalist prick. I raised cows in the pastures, felled trees in the woods, and hoarded the hearts of farmers' daughters. I was every sort of real champion. I was one with my country, my great nation. God bless her sweet, self-justifying beauty.

Out fishin the local crick, word got out about me. As it goes, people know not to interrupt anytime I'm slaying some trout. So I wasn't interrupted. I was out there all the live long day. At least they had that much of decency in themselves. Though maybe they looked and just couldn't find me. I was way out. Like my fishin holes tend to be.

Back at the town meetin hall, I'd posted up a notice. It said simply enough, "I'm done with the damn lot of you. It's one thing after another you hold against this country, to the point I can see how you just hate it outright. Why don't you ever just say so? You know it's true. So starting right now, I want you all out. Come on, you know you hate this great land, so just get out. Go on, move along." And I added in bold and underlined: "Best you just leave now before I make ya."

I signed it, "Crazy Cass," which is what they call me, just for my convictions, I guess.

I'd been stewing to myself all this time. Saying things in my head like, "You hate this country that I love, so I hate you!" I had to cool off. You know, that's why I took the day and went fishin.

I was hoping by the time I got back, every one of them irritating bastards would be gone. But a part of me knew it wouldn't be so easy.

This place draws a lot of unintelligent people. When folks of that sort engage in civil righteousness, they get uppity. Their instincts are all off the mark, of course. Right away what they do is, they raise battle cries.

I made it back to town at a slow pace. My stewing was all done. Thanks to the river. That almighty, unstoppable rushing of glacial waters. Going away to the ocean. Taking with it my angriest thoughts and washing clean the pure form of patriotic goodness. All with a big trout to show for my efforts.

Coming up to my place, same time as when I was getting there, was the sheriff. His name is Gerald and his wife is more religious than most. Pastor says he, Gerald, is godless, and I wouldn't doubt it. I wouldn't doubt that one bit. How their dinner prayers must go, is just a trauma even to think about.

Sheriff says, "Cass... Well, hello, Cass..."

I can't help thinking at that moment how he's just a sinner and an atheist, hardly a man at all. So I give a gruff non-meaningful shake of the head.

"Cass," says the sheriff, "what's this about posting threats at the meetin hall?"

"I don't post threats," I tell him. "Not me. If you seen my message posted up, that's because it was a vigilante notification. A kind of just lettin y'all know." Here I nodded again and it was meaningful this time. "Just lettin y'all know."

"Call it what you like, but that threat you posted up today has got some folks worried. Not just worried, but upset that someone would ever think to do harm to others around here. To impose upon another's way of life. It's a small community, Cass. Real close-knit. We help each other out. That's what we do. We don't go pushin others around. That's not the right way to get things done."

"Between you and me, Gerald," I said, feeling the weight of the dinner I held in my arms, "I'd rather just go in and cook up a nice trout."

He let me walk by. Up the steps of my house. I went inside and next time I looked, he was gone.

The battle cries came a bit later. First there was something else. A knock at my door in the evening and I went to go see. There was no one, only a letter there on the mat. It said, "No, YOU leave, you nationalist prick!" That's all. It wasn't signed.

I had a trout and a beer for dinner. Watched some sports. Worked a little bit on the coffee table I'm building. I do a little wood working on the side. Next I'll be working on a clock if I can get the table to turn out.

Around eleven it was about time for bed. But first I still had to shower off and say prayers. Been thinkin too much lately about them farmers' daughters, so you know I had plenty to pray about.

Right in the middle of showerin I could hear their battle cries. They weren't really raising battle cries, not at that moment, but as I say—in my thoughts and prayers it was sure like as though they were raising them. God as my witness. For if the thoughts in my mind matter even one bit, sure enough God could hear it, too.

I toweled off and was rearin to go. It's possible I had a pinch of the whiskey bottle, with the thought of it helping with gettin to sleep. And then I had some more, and instead of gettin to bed, I grabbed hold of my shotgun and went out into the street.

It's a love of country that goes above all else. Always been so. Well, no, church first, then country. Though, the way I see it is, you love the one, you love the other.

With my shotgun in hand and all revved up, I went out to the old town hall and just started firin. Took shots up into the sky. Took em this way and the other. Said, "I'll give y'all a count of ten to get on outta here! A count of ten. And then I start a shootin to hit somethin!"

I reloaded in a hurry so I'd be ready. For my country, my great country. The place I was born and raised. The place where freedom rings and God is good. Where you can get up and know if you work hard, well, you've made it. Because this country is yours, if you'll have it. So just don't go a hatin on it, you know?

Nothin happened so I sat down and figured I'd just come too early for the showdown, that's all. I had my countdown ready for the moment it was needed. Soon as the town people showed themselves. All the while, in the back of my mind, I could hear their battle cries coming at me.

"Peace not war!" was one.

"End gun violence!" was another.

"Down with nationalist pricks!" was a third and especially loud one.

There were others. All whirling around my head. I had my whiskey bottle with me, thank the Lord. I gave out a prayer in thanks. Then I took a few big gulps and by some miracle still had half a full bottle left. It's times like this you know how God is good.

"Put the bottle down, Cass. Just put it down."

I looked around with bleary eyes and couldn't see a thing. Except the angel of the Lord come down with bright lights and all shining upon me. But it was only the sheriff, Gerald. Shouting at me from his patrol car with high beams on.

"Go to hell, sheriff!" I yelled back. But he'd already got me by the arms. The bottle slipped and crashed. I struggled for my rifle but my hands already were cuffed. Nothing would stop me, not by the grace of God, I thought. Then took one on the jaw and hit the pavement, last thing I knew.

In jail as the sun rose up, I looked down at these hands and these feet of mine. Tugged at my beard and gave my neck a scratch. Had some real thinkin to do. I had every right to be a nationalist prick. I grew crops in the valleys, drove trucks across the land, got baptized in the glacial waters.

But this nationalist prick business was not for me. It was for someone else, sure, but not for me. I was meant for the quiet of the hills, deeper on into the woods, apart from these strange times. I was too pure, in a way, too much a monument and a threat, like a grizzly bear is a threat. I told this to God, but kept one thing back for myself. My thoughts of the farmers' daughters. I'd keep on holding them close to my heart, if they'd have me.

TROPHY #JAILBAIT

"Greetings from the fair!" Picture of us holding ice cream cones kneeling down next to a goat named Edgar.

After posting this, a lot of things started happening.

"I'm taking the goat," said Missy.

"You're drunk!" I laughed.

I was trying to find my wife; she was trying to find her parents. I was drunk, too, and wanted to run off with her. I might have said this out loud.

Trumpets and trombones drowned out everything for a second. Couldn't tell where from. Behind the cows?

"Edgar + Missy 4 ev!" Picture of Missy lifting the goat over the fence, ice cream gone in teeth—

goat shooting out tongue just shy of licking ice cream.

All at once, I realized this crazy chicka was serious about taking the goat. Okay, well, maybe goats are good at sniffing out wives or parents? Aren't all animals instinctual and good for something?

We made a run for it. I was pretty sweaty to begin with. It was great to move faster than the flies buzzing around my head.

Felicia my wife said she'd call after the stupid arts and crafts exhibit. I totally knew she'd sneak in a deep-fried Twinkie without me. Still, she could call after a reasonable time. A guy shouldn't have to employ a pubescent angel girl and steal a goat to—

Phone! Phone! Phone!

These weren't calls but photo-likes coming in. Even a few comments:

"Score!!!"

"Hell yeah tap that a$$ son!"

"Titties! #JailbaitTitties!"

That's what's great about life. Everybody appreciates a great pair of tits if you can find some. Everybody does!

Picture of me licking ice cream off awesome cleavage close up.

She pulled out a cool glass pipe. Where'd she get that? While toking up, she flicked off the camera. Bad ass!

Then we lost the goat. Just great, I thought, no wife, no parents, now no goat. It just goes to show one truth I've found time and time again. If there is a god, she is funny as hell! Like Christians I know who say sometimes: just look at the platypus! Isn't it ridiculous?! You've got to be a weirdo to make that!

I can personally say that the banana is a pretty damn good proof of god: you just peel it away and that's food? Come on, that's cool!

Go ahead and dip that shit in chocolate and then deep fry it and dip it again and freeze it? Then mush it all up, add sprinkles, drizzle syrup, and eat it with a spoon? How is that even possible unless it's god?

My eyes rolled back into my head. Evidently I wasn't the only one thinking about bananas. Here behind a random t-shirt stand she'd discovered my personal banana of sorts and got hold of it with her lips and tongue.

Phone! Phone! Phone!
"Look it's the fountain of youth!"
"Niagara Falls #Jailbait!"
"Hahaha, yer fucked!"
"Them titties tho!"

That's pretty great. People love anything behind the scenes. People love people. My eyes could see so far into my brain I could die.

Back to business, I took off her shirt for good as we climbed up the sides of the World's Tallest Bungee Jump Tower to about a hundred feet or so. This way we'd really be able to see where her parents went to. Also the goat. Also my wife!

Thinking back to when little sweet Missy had gulped down all my drinks at the bikini bar in exchange for gropes of her body anywhere I wanted, thinking back as diligent as possible, I couldn't remember who'd been responsible for finishing off the most number of drinks. Was it six or ten someone had, or fourteen? One of those was definitely a familiar number, or was one of those just somebody's age or shoe size?

By this time we'd scaled the great tower! I held her in my arms! She climbed onto my shoulders, danced on my head!

"I don't really have any parents," she cried.

"That's okay," I cried back. "My wife Felicia? No comment!"

Off in the distance, the goat was escaping, high tailing it through the parking lot and almost home free.

You make it past that shopping mall, then a few miles of tracts of suburban developments, then you're back out in the wild. Up here, I could see the edges of civilization on all sides.

"Hey, how old are you anyway? You look like you could be my dad!"

"Ha, ha! Who cares? You first!"

"Twenty-three!"

"Huh? Thank god! I was worried you might be—"

Picture of us from the top of the world with that crowd below, seen from a few thousand cameras and a helicopter circling, news stations everywhere saying they finally found so and so from the most wanted list, and Missy slipping off and away to a chorus of screams.

"Swan dive titties!"

"Trophy #jailbait!"

"She dead!"

ACE VENTURA: SLEEPY DOOMSDAY

"I'm the landlord of the artist lofts and I decide who's woke a.f. and who's not. It's my ballpark, fuckboiz."

We got this note on the door and figured it was all over for us. All our mountains of art would have to be put into storage. We'd have to go our separate ways, find normal apartments in the sleepy a.f. burbs just like all the other fuckboiz gone before us. We just didn't realize it would all happens so quickly.

*

"Citizens! Must be content to reduce complex dynamic issues world views and beliefs into ready made slogans! #community #weouthere #wokeboiz" said the landlord on social media that fateful day.

"Subsidize me, Captain," said Will, the only ironic or post-ironic one left of our little artist troupe.

Will was working on a giant mural across the entire face of the building. Couldn't tell what it was yet but it looked a hell of a lot like Ace Ventura.

Then the landlord showed up with his buddies the cops.

"These are the fuckboiz I was telling you about," he said.

"Okay rats, scum, losers, and fuckboiz," said one of the cops, "form a single file line starting right here."

We all lined up.

"Strip!" said the cop.

We stripped.

"Dance around making animal noises, brawl, kiss each other's asses, or, you know, do whatever you can think of to dehumanize yourselves!"

The usual.

"Fill this out!" said the cop, handing around the official Woke Test from the Woke Officers' Krime Enforcement (WOKE) Agency.

We filled it out.

*

That night, we all returned as disenfranchised homeless graffiti artists and helped Will complete his Ace Ventura mural. Ace Ventura, the least woke person or symbol of a person to ever live (according to an official WOKE report on woke krimes).

Even before we had a chance to finish, as the sun came up, the wrecking balls started flying. The cops had discovered the mural. No more artist lofts. :(

But the wrecking crew didn't stop there. The main wrecking ball guy turned out to be the landlord. His wrecking ball just kept swinging while he shouted various accusations and #wokeslogans:

"Take this for judging being hateful mean and lame to others fuckboiz!" and "Get the bigots out of my wokelyfe!" and "Fuck you everybody everyone and everything!"

Pretty soon the whole town was leveled. I guess it just wasn't woke enough. Oh well. Now the whole place is sleepy a.f. for real.

DR. HOLOGRAM

I sneeze holograms, I explained while ordering a burrito.

"Always pinup girls?" asked the guy taking my order. He lifted his baseball cap out of his eyes and gawked. The girl—semi-translucent, like partly from a dream—jiggled her hips by the beer fridge, as if trying to slip out of her tiny red bikini, no hands.

I shrugged.

"Can I keep her?"

"Sure," I shrugged again.

"Bless you, by the way."

"Thanks."

I took a seat at one of the bright yellow tables outside, shaded from the sun by an extravagant straw umbrella. It was festive in a sort of cheap, careless way—just right for this afternoon. While waiting for my burrito, I enjoyed my chips, salsa, and Mexican beer.

I had officially completed my dissertation for my tenth Ph.D. Ten of them. Wow. I was celebrating.

It bummed me out, really, seeing Roxanne like that. It had been about two Ph.Ds. ago. That long? Must have been. But there she was in a burrito joint in San Francisco, dancing gleefully out of step with the radio mariachi music, swinging her translucent limbs all over the salsa bar as a holographic pinup girl.

Not only did she have an aversion to education, she had bad taste in guys. I found that out when she went back to her previous boyfriend. She wrote me to say that she secretly had panic attacks whenever I brought up artificial superintelligence (which I was studying). Shortly after that, I saw a picture of her and her man. He was a sight. Backwards hat, skeleton tattoo on his neck. Totally one-dimensional. Probably worked as a test subject for lab experiments, same as Roxanne.

But lord she looked fine in that lollipop red bikini top in there. White scarf-thing (silk) tied around her hips. Smiling. Taking her sunglasses off and dancing as though walking like a princess over hot beach sand.

"Number eighty-two?"

I looked at my receipt. "Yeah," I said. He already knew—was already setting my burrito in front of me. Good at what he did. A series of tasks—

swatting them aside as they came at him. Never really accomplishing anything. Just tasks. Seriously inferior to any robot doing the same thing.

But we like people. We like how they walk among us. Don't we? Yes—especially when they stay out of our way.

I had a thought.

"Hey—uh...!"

"Yes?"

"Is she still in there?"

"She?"

"The girl—the pinup girl..."

His face scrunched up under his baseball cap—a working man's smile—and he started he say something, but stopped himself just before a bad joke came out. His laugh was a "yes."

"When you get a chance—"

He was already walking away! —That's why: the people at the other table were hailing him. Another task for him. Now multiple tasks. Look at him trying to juggle them! He's looking at the people at the other table, also glancing at me.

"Number..." He said, loud enough for everyone to hear, leaning over the table, studying their receipt. "Number eighty-three!"

A few weeks ago I would have been taking last-minute notes for my latest thesis (cognitive holographic fabrication). But now I didn't really care to watch. I could forget about observing real people and thinking about holograms for a while. I was already moving onto the next thing (holography superintelligence—unknown territory).

So much knowledge, and knowledge is power. So much power.

But now was a time to take a break. Relax. Celebrate!

The baseball cap guy came back to me, still grinning. I liked him. He was here to please. He seemed to have an enjoyment for these tasks, giving in to the fact that they were inevitable. Giving meaning to them as an extension of their inevitability.

"When you get a chance," I said, continuing my thought from before, "can you see if she wants to come out here?"

"The pinup?"

I nodded.

"Sure, I'll see," he gave me a chummy nudge.

"Thanks—her name's Roxanne."

"Roxanne? Okay."

"Yeah. She may not know that. Actually...I'm not sure..."

He just kept nodding and walked away. Would she know her name? Well, never mind. It was probably a mistake, anyway. Probably better to just leave her be, swaying her hips to increase beer sales.

Sometimes you do things in life because you love the pursuit of education. Other times you have a morbid curiosity.

I ate some chips, enjoying the variety of salsas at my disposal, intending to clear my mind (to make her go away), but instead, thinking:

When I set out to study holograms, I promised myself I'd never abuse my powers. I'd keep a healthy academic indifference about it. When I implanted myself with the hologram maker, nothing was supposed to change. I'd become a little more god-like, sure, but I'd still have my academic principles guiding me.

This glitch with the sneezes made things more complicated—albeit more interesting. Sneezes, evidently, are tied precariously to our passions. The idea was to manifest holograms with the mind after a period of premeditation—not spontaneously with a sneeze! It's the passionate connection tied to sneezes that create these holograms that strain, shall we say, one's sense of academic purity.

And wouldn't you know it. The moment you graduate and lose your university funding, allergy season hits.

Maybe it was something in the salsa—more likely it was the pollen. But I felt another sneeze coming on. I thought maybe I could blink it away, but this one was a freight train. It came on fast and hard, no way I could stop it.

I looked around, expecting the worst.

"Bless you," said the lady at the table behind me.

That wasn't so bad, I thought. It was just a harmless sneeze. It felt pretty good, actually. That release. Nothing like a champion sneeze before a good meal!

Then I noticed how I suddenly had two burritos. Ah. I laughed vaguely. For the life of me, I couldn't tell which one was real...!

I was going in for the smell test when a hand reached under my nose and picked up the nearest burrito.

"Hi, Charlie!" said Roxanne, taking the seat across from me with the holographic burrito in hand. "How's the salsa?"

I smirked at her. She always looked fine as a human. But as a hologram—wow!

My mind quickly went to just where you'd expect. While she was here, why not make it a strip tease?

Oh God!!!

I didn't mean to. Sometimes, thoughts slip. That's what happened with her top—it just slipped right off.

You know those moments when—well, basically, you get caught looking at porn? That was how I felt. Like the whole burrito joint had caught me. Like I was sitting here indulging in visual pleasures in public, inviting all of San Francisco to laugh at what I apparently found to be so amazingly arousing that I couldn't help myself!

Roxanne was oblivious, of course, sitting there eating her burrito, delightedly humming a tune, now and then bobbing her shoulders in rhythm to her humming. And her breasts, shiny in the sunlight, unfortunately, looked great.

My face was bright red. I tried not to stare, as if that would make any difference. I'd really have to focus to make her go away. But maybe it wouldn't hurt to ask.

"It looks like your—uh—your top came off, there. Do you think you could...?"

"My top?"

"Yeah."

She looked down at her naked breasts, kind of studied them, then smiled vacantly. I leaned forward enough to see that the top hadn't only fallen off—it had vanished.

I had to get rid of her, fast. But I simply couldn't focus. Also I felt another sneeze coming on. Worst of all, it was like she could read my thoughts.

"Being afraid of spontaneous creation is like being afraid of yourself," she said.

I looked around to see if anyone had noticed my under-dressed companion. Some guy across the street opened his window and appeared to be enjoying the view with a camera in hand. A few people walked by gawking, but kept their thoughts to themselves. Thank God for civilized drone-types. The types of people who don't make scenes are the only ones who truly keep this planet spinning (no thanks to me—sitting here inviting scenes to be made).

"What's the matter, anyway?" she persisted (now in my voice!). "Haven't you written doctoral theses on virtually every advancement of the future of consciousness, technology, and the human species? Don't you have some idea how this is all going to turn out?"

Ironically, that gave me an idea (as I held in a sneeze).

"Speaking of artificial superintelligence," I said in my scholarly tone she hated, "I was just reading how we could reach the point of singularity any day now."

She gave me a disapproving look, just as I expected. Keep this up and she'd vanish out of sight in no time, I figured.

"At that point," I continued, "the AI will be as intelligent and autonomous as the smartest and most capable human being—it'll be a walking, talking Einstein: artificial, but with emotional intelligence and everything. But it's intelligence won't stop there. It will continue to learn, since it's programmed to learn by itself. The smartest human has an IQ of about one-hundred sixty. Within a matter of days after reaching singularity, the AI may reach an IQ of nine-hundred. Then one thousand. Then three thousand!"

"Why do you always have to bring this up?" Roxanne complained, using her own voice again. She was shaking, taking quick, shallow breaths, just as she used to.

There was a police car at the intersection. When the light changed, they would drive past. No way they wouldn't notice. Even in San Francisco, cops can't help themselves about making scenes over public nudity. I had to hurry.

"It's impossible to tell what could happen if a being with that sort of power lived among us. It would be like God. It would cure cancer, solve all the mysteries of science for us. But also it might find that we stand in the way of some greater purpose. It might—"

"Hey, chicka... Ow, ow!" A group of bros came out of the burrito joint. Great! Their eyes were popping out of their heads as they came right towards us.

Roxanne was still shaking, looking at me, and the horny bros were hollering louder than ever when the police car pulled up alongside the curb. I panicked.

"The world is going to end!" I yelled at Roxanne. "Artificial superintelligence is going to take control and destroy everything! I know—I have ten Ph.Ds.!"

The bros backed away a little, but the cops were charging.

Just then the pollen—or the salsa—was too much for me. I let out a machine gun fire of sneezes, each one more overpowering than the last.

"Number eighty-three?" said the guy in the baseball cap, coming out with his arms full of burritos.

"Bless you!" said the lady at the table behind me, this time irritably (as she accepted her burrito). I kept sneezing.

Everyone fell silent for one terrible moment, right as I was between giant sneezes, sucking in air to fill my lungs for the next bout of machine gun fire. Then someone gasped.

One of the cops mumbled, "What the hell?" as I fell off my seat onto the sidewalk, sweating, trying to hold my nose between explosions.

The sky darkened. I looked up through watery eyes to see a massive hologram spaceship hovering over, casting not only a shadow, but also shooting beams of darkness (like the opposite of spotlights) over the whole city. The base of the ship opened up and robotic creatures began descending upon us like a swarm of satanic bees.

By this time, my sneezes had let up, but the damage was done. Everyone was screaming, crying, or dropping onto their knees to pray or beg for mercy or something. The cops were doing their bests to recover from their initial shock. One of them was mumbling into his radio while the other crouched beside the police car, taking aim and firing at the various holographic monsters coming down from the sky.

"See?" said a voice in my mind. "It's not very funny, is it?"

I looked around and noticed a guy, like fate, stomping right towards me. It was a hologram of Roxanne's boyfriend—neck tattoo and all. He was all huffed up in a rage—over two hundred pounds of brute-force stupidity.

"See what you've done! See what you've done!" he bellowed, clenching his fists, pounding his chest.

Roxanne ran to him, burrowing her naked body against his sweat-stained t-shirt. She glared at me accusingly. "All that learning," she said, "for *what*? The end of the goddamn world?"

I sat back in my seat, ate a chip, took a big bite of my burrito, sipped some beer. A cool breeze ran down my neck. Not bad, I thought, enjoying the show.

PAROLE OFFICER PETE

I'm just wired different. Never fails to get me busted. One time my parole officer summed me up perfect. "You think you can get away with anything, huh?" he said.

Walking down the street, I waited for myself to pick up a rock and throw it into the windshield of a passing car. That would have been my answer, "Yes sir, I do." But no cars passed and they must have recently cleaned the sidewalk because there weren't any rocks to throw.

My parole officer is my best friend Pete. And my name is Pete. We're just two guys named Pete.

Pete has a brand new wife and she takes him to church twice a week. It's some very kinky sort of foreplay as far as he's concerned. He likes the idea that God can watch over his most private thoughts and actions.

That's what it's like to be wired right. When you think you can't get away with anything.

I figured I'd go ahead and kill Pete so there'd be one less guy for God to spy on. But I didn't know where he lived—only where he went to church.

Standing outside his church, I looked at all the young girls walking by in their dresses and skirts. It started to make sense that I was just like God—just watching and waiting.

Then Pete came along. He held his wife in one hand and his Bible in the other. Totally weighed down on both sides.

He walked right by. If he noticed me, he didn't show it. So why did I have to notice him?

I waited for myself to burn the church down. But it was my last day on parole and I didn't have any matches.

META WITH DAVE

I can only study the brain for so long. Most of my co-workers love nothing more than to slice off thin layers of cortex like making a sandwich. I've never seen anyone take a scalpel to brain tissue without giggling and salivating.

Here's this grey/pink chunk right here. Know what that is? That's Dave. He had a wife and two kids. Divorced in his late fifties and spent most of his sixties traveling around betting on golf courses. He was the most upstanding person from Las Vegas I've ever known.

I never actually met the guy. But the second I got his brain, I did a quick search to see the type of specimen we were dealing with. His Facebook page was still active. He had a lot of pictures. Here's one of his posts:

There's nothing more sensuous
than to hear: retroactive salary payment.

Not completely sure what he's talking about there. Here's one with a personal touch:
Dinner with friends from 30 years ago.
Bring on 3 more decades of shenanigans!

His liver wasn't much good. Nor were his lungs. Most of his organs were incinerated with the rest of his body. But I'm told his kidneys were quite salvageable and here, of course, we have his brain.

In there, a galaxy of neurons was frozen in the dance of consciousness. With all this machinery more or less intact, you'd think it would be possible to start 'er up again. Jumpstart this old grey Jello with some kind of voodoo chant and get the old boy talking again.

"Hi! I do real estate investments and golf on the weekends... God, how fortunate am I to be blessed with these two kids, even if they're brats! ...Ah, my guts! My poor ass! ...Yeah, hit with a dose of colon cancer. It's out of control. It's the iceberg and my body's the Titanic. Ship's going down. Last game of golf, I guess, then off to catch something real nasty from the best-looking escort in Vegas. What the hell, you know? Wish me luck!"

I took a slice out of his cortex. "Not a bad looking slab of brain you got there, Dave," I said.

"Not bad? Damn, Rob, that's looking primo!"

It was Dr. Meyers with a steak knife. Passing through the lab, he took a generous slice of Dave, slapped it between two pieces of bread, and went out to join everyone on lunch break.

I threw off my gloves with a shrug. Needing a break myself, I took a small slice and joined the others in the cafeteria.

SOUTHSIDE PARK

Got ahold of some cheap street chalk. With my buddy Mark, went to Southside Park. It's the Sacramento place to be homeless and either Catholic, Muslim, or Buddhist, judging by the big ugly churches that border the park on all sides.

"Ready to go do your thing?" Mark asked over a pre-game coffee.

"What thing?"

"With the chalk."

"Ah, yeah. There's no thing—just all this chalk."

"So what's it for?"

"I'll show ya."

Who says you need a plan. Better to roll without one. Got to be ready to shift and adapt. Plans can only fuck up a perfect day of spontaneously making the world more beautiful.

At Southside we found a place in the middle of the park partly shaded but still a little sunny. A few homeless guys getting drunk and hoping to sell some crystal meth sat by watching.

I started off with my trademark image, the Purple Bowtie Monster Man, and Mark drew the picture closest to his heart, a cartoon toilet with a thought bubble, "Don't shit on me!"

Next I drew my best guess at a satanic symbol and Mark drew a traditional upside-down cross with the unambiguous phrase, "Hail Satan!" Now we were getting somewhere!

It's freaking hard being funny under pressure. You can't do a chalk drawing in a park and have it be lame. The worst thing ever is a public display of a lack of imagination.

"I got one!" I said.

About fifty seconds later, bam: Buddha with a crack pipe.

"Awesome!" said Mark, and he's not easily impressed.

"Okay, I got one," said Mark, getting down on his knees like a professional.

He outdid himself with this one: Osama Bin Laden with big titties and a stunted dick and balls.

"That's so good!" I laughed, not knowing how I would ever top that.

I kept at it with a picture of a stick figure pissing. I was still trying to figure out what he should be pissing on when a kinda ghetto woman stopped and screamed at us, "Hey, you know little kids walk through here!"

As if to prove her point, right at her heels was a herd of fast-food-eating little brats. They looked shabby and wily but at least you couldn't say undernourished.

We just ignored the lady and her posse of juveniles. Obviously kids need to learn things at some point. Also...kids know! They know who're the good guys vs. the bad guys. They know well enough this lady is the bad guy and we're the champions.

Unhappy that she was ignored, the lady erased Osama Bin Laden's titties and dick by pouring water all over the picture.

God, that hurt!

We let her take her anger out. No sweat. Let her be that person everyone hates. She's necessary. It's cool. She has to do that. Like Jacques the Fatalist would say, it was written up yonder.

We carried on drawing more vigorously than ever and I hardly even noticed the rise in activity in the park. Church had let out...

I was slaving away at the following work: a gargantuan talking hamburger speaking the classic Shakespeare quote, "Peace, ye fat guts!" Just then a group of elderly Buddhists came up behind me, belligerent as hell. I couldn't figure out if they were speaking English or what. Evidently they were pissed about my Buddha with the crack pipe.

When Mark and I snubbed their belligerence, they started spitting heavily on my artwork. Who knew Buddhists had so much damn spit inside themselves!

Pretty soon, my Buddha looked like a sloppy, pixelated Cartman at best.

By that time, the Catholics, the Muslims, more Buddhists, and a bunch of non-affiliated overweight mothers had gathered. Mark and I could barely keep up creating art and beauty as quickly as it was being destroyed by one ill-advised idiot or another.

Thank fucking god for the kids. That's who came to our aid! Jesus, and I thought I was a pervert. Those kids, armed with chalk, were like next level John Waters Minis! I swear I'd never seen so many dicks and balls, pussies, middle fingers, defaced religious symbols, etc. in multicolored chalk!

There was hatred projected at police officers, teachers, political figures; there was fun poked at the mass media, terrorists, poverty, drugs, dumb governments, schoolyard bullies; most of all, there was lots of lust for sex, carnage, and money.

Most kids, I'll admit, started out with pictures of hearts and flowers and smiley faces. But these kids, I knew right away, were independent thinkers if I'd ever seen any. When no one was looking, they'd sneak a hand down their pants or up their nose and scribble an explicit sex aphorism they couldn't possibly have understood.

This went on all day, us and the innocent youth warring in silent chalk pics against the religious authorities and parents of Southside Park.

Everything was going cool until the original ghetto woman went over to score some crystal meth from the homeless populace. A homeless drunk guy she approached stood up, suddenly huge and burly and mean. Right away, things soured. The woman was throwing crap out of her purse and yelling how someone owed her money. Then the homeless guy threw off his homeless man coat. Oh shit—he was a cop!

"Serves her damn right," said Mark as the cop brought out the cuffs.

"That's what you get for being all high minded about art on a beautiful day," I agreed.

"Dude, I think I'm out of chalk," Mark said a minute later.

"Me too," I said. "Plus, I'm starved."

"Screw this place. Let's get some burritos."

All the homeless guys in the park started throwing off their coats. Turned out they were all cops the whole time. I guess everyone probably got busted for something. God bless America, brother. What a shit show!

SAM'S HANG GLIDER DIVE BOMBS

Light fog forming today off the coast in Daly City, CA, and Jethro's up there someplace. I was perched on the roof of the Korean Baptist Church, right on the edge of a cliff overlooking the Pacific. A little chilled, a little bored, but always keeping a watchful eye. This neighborhood and the San Francisco Peninsula would not be terrorized today, not if I could help it.

A friendly guy named Larry called up from the church entrance.

"God bless you, Sam!"

And his wife cheered me on.

"Keeping you in our prayers, honey!"

I don't do anything to invite these remarks; then again, I don't mind them, either.

Jethro thinks he owns the coast, but he doesn't. I fired him long ago from the Pacifica Hang Gliders' Hobby Shop. Know what he did to get fired? I'll tell you. He disparaged customers. The best intentioned, most loyal, most faithful customers in the world were chased off in a matter of weeks.

He also stole. I didn't find that out until later, but he stole a lot. I was never too good at keeping books.

Right after I fired him, he said, "Tonight, sundown, Korean Baptist Church on the cliff. Be there."

This was a threat. His show-off way of trying to intimidate me. I didn't show up. That was my way of saying, "I'm the one in charge here, not you, punk."

For a few weeks after that, silence. My customers started coming back. Business returned to normal, with daily hang glider rentals, guided outings, and merch sales so high I almost missed Jethro handling all the customer-facing activities.

I put up a new job ad: "Customer service specialist needed in local hobby shop. Enthusiasm for all things hang-glider-centric a must. So, if you love hang gliders, this is the job for you. Downtown Pacifica, by the pier. Full time. Hourly wage negotiable based on years of experience in hang glider industry."

Then I got Jessica helping out. What was I ever thinking with Jethro, anyway? I should have just waited for Jessica to come along. She was exactly the customer service specialist I'd been waiting for! Even though she had never actually been hang gliding (scared of heights and didn't particularly fantasize about the ways of birds), I figured that didn't matter much so long as she never told this to customers.

At the Pacifica Hang Gliders' Hobby Shop, we do one thing: promote high quality goods and services for the hang glider enthusiast in all of us (even Jessica, I believe—I should add that she's only 18, so she's got plenty of time to come around).

Perched atop the crest of the Korean Baptist Church, I often stare out towards the sunset, wishing I could see a sunset, but usually there's just fog. Just layers of this cold, haunting shroud, turning the day's end into a characterless disappointment. Down below, in the church parking lot, a group of smiling Koreans often sing a hymn in my honor. I wave down at them and bow as best I can with my glider on my back.

I started hearing rumors that Jethro was recruiting people. Mostly drunks and washed up folks from the heavy metal crowd at Winter's Tavern. I told Jessica to be careful.

The next day, my hobby shop got robbed. According to Jessica, a mob of masked men raided the store out of nowhere. They knew what they wanted and they took it. They took just about everything. The police said they'd be on the case, but I doubted their ability to do much.

"Jethro did this," I said, standing in the midst of the desolated hobby shop, my pride and joy.

"Are you sure?" Jessica asked. Her innocence was unbelievable, and I suppose I liked that.

"Yes. Only he would do something like this."

I needed a shoulder to cry on. I don't know what got into me. This wasn't something I had ever intended to tell anyone.

"Jessica?"

"Yeah?"

"This might sound crazy, but Jethro is the best damn hang glider I've ever seen."

"Is he really that good?"

"I'm afraid so."

Not long after the store robbery, a small group of novice hang gliders were attacked near Thornton State Beach. Masked hang gliders appeared out of a fogbank. Unprovoked, they started dive-bombing the novices. Ominous cries for help could be heard throughout the Westlake neighborhood. But the fog had quickly become too thick for anyone to see the assault taking place.

The victims were driven away from the coast where they finally spiraled into the ocean beyond the breakers.

I heard all about it that same evening when the novices returned to my shop drenched and shell-shocked. Their rented equipment had all been destroyed in the crash and was washed out to sea.

I helped them file a police report. The loss of equipment was another major blow to my bottom line.

The next victims were a group of hotshot hobbyists from Los Angeles. Same story. Out of the evening fogbank, masked gliders came dive-bombing. Even the hotshots didn't stand a chance against the masked gang.

After that it seemed clear that no one was safe. The gang went on to attack a few first-time surfers in Pacifica; they terrorized horseback riders near Fort Funston; they taunted golfers at the Olympic Club; they terrorized innocent families at Ocean Beach by stealing little kids' kites; they even pelted the Korean church-goers with handfuls of tiny dead crabs.

Things quieted down briefly toward the end of July. But then I heard reports that similar instances had started happening in Southern California and even down along the Baja Peninsula.

I knew that Jethro needed to be stopped. He was giving the pastime of hang gliding a truly terrible name and ruining it for everyone.

"We haven't had any business all week," Jessica reminded me sadly.

"It's only Thursday," I said.

She smiled bleakly, saddened further by my pathetic optimism.

I would have sent Jessica home but she was only there for the money. I didn't want to deprive her of that.

"How about you and me take a quick flight—just to catch the sunset."

"Alright," she answered, probably to escape the boredom and the hopelessness of her day up to that point.

We gathered up all the scraps of equipment I had left in my shop and headed to the bluff off Skyline Boulevard.

"If things get any worse, we may both be out of a job!" I laughed, trying to lighten the mood.

She was staring up at some birds flying down the coast.

"Is it scary?"

"Not to those birds."

"They're in their element."

"So they would make lousy humans. Unlike them, we thrive by exploring outside our natural element."

"Is that your argument for hang gliding?"

"Watch this..."

It took me a few minutes to get all harnessed up, but then I was off. The ground gave way as my glider gripped the force of the breeze. Woo! I felt that rush of flight. In that moment, you wonder right away why people don't do this all the time.

Down below, Jessica clapped her hands and laughed. It was the first time I'd seen her do a real outdoorsy smile.

My hobby shop policy strictly prohibits falling in love with employees. Good thing. I would have really hated to fall for Jess. From that outdoors smile of hers, I could tell she was a heartbreaker.

Sometimes my inner flirt still gets the better of me. I wondered if she'd get scared if I flew into the fogbank and disappeared for a moment. The wind was pushing me that way anyway.

The world grew hushed and it immediately felt like dusk. This was the fogbank. Thick as pea soup, for sure.

Just then I heard a scream.

"Jessica!" I shouted.

My voice didn't seem to travel far. I veered back to the coast, shivering as a dark shadow whizzed by. My next thought: Jethro...! I barely had a moment to think before I was struck from behind by an incredible force. The very next instant, something came down upon me from above, knocking me into a summersault.

Jessica's scream came again but this time from a different direction. Or was I just disoriented? Either way, I would never have made it back to the coast in one piece. I was going down fast. Just like that, my body slammed against the surface of the freezing salt water.

The sudden shock filled my entire body with an incredible rage. It's possible I could have drowned. But there's no way that would have happened. Instead of looking death in the face, I found myself wondering how people could ever possibly die. The pure adrenaline flowing through me would have kept me alive through anything. If a shark had seen me then, he would have panicked and chewed off its own tail in fear.

I hadn't breathed in a while. Tangled under a mass of colorful fabric and metal, it was like the broken hang glider was trying to force feed me to the ocean.

Jethro had all but ruined my life. Who did he think he was, anyway? If he ever laid a finger on Jessica, I'd…

My superhuman adrenaline rush lasted just long enough for me to scrambled out from under the deathtrap hang glider. That first gasp of breath was the greatest catharsis I'd ever known. Flopping my limbs and sputtering, my next thought was to cry for help. The fogbank rolled over me as I kicked and splashed my way back to the shore. If any sharks turned away, it was just out of pity.

I told the cops what happened, for whatever that was worth.

The next day, there was a story in the paper that included a direct quote by me: "When Jethro swoops in for the kill, someone's going down!" That set the tone for the story. It was treated like a big joke.

When Jessica didn't show up to work the next day, I closed up shop at noon. There hadn't been any customers anyway. I went to get coffee at the Chit Chat Café off Manor Drive. No one there had heard anything about the possible whereabouts of Jethro or his gang. I went online and found a few articles about the recent terrorism of the rogue hang gliders. Reports were coming in from all the way up and down the coast.

I tend to get paranoid when caffeinated. Every worst-case scenario flitted through my mind. Especially unsettling was the fact that I was partly responsible for creating this Jethro monster.

Jess called.

"Don't go back to your shop," she said in a whisper.

"Where are you?"

"At my parents' house. I'm fine. Just don't go back to the shop, okay?"

"You mean right now, or in general?"

"In general. So, just don't ever go back. Jethro has already taken it over. He'll send you an offer to buy it. Just accept his offer. It's all you can do."

"How do I know you're really at your parents' house?"

"I have to go."

"Okay."

I walked back to the beach. Scraps of my hang glider had washed up along with about a million tiny dead crabs. Broken and dead things almost always wash up. I took the scraps back to my house. In my garage, I got all my best scraps out and set to work. I was up all night. The sun rose and I felt like a million bucks. I kept at it.

By noon, it was time for a trial run with my brand new glider. I took it up and almost fell asleep in the air. Landing sloppily, nearly crashing into the bluff, I took a nap on a secret beach. When I awoke, I hadn't eaten all day and the sun was beginning to set.

For a treat, I drove down to Gorilla BBQ. While eating a big plate of beef with mac and cheese, I pieced together the horrible reality of the Jethro situation and I tried to figure out what to do next. What did Jethro ultimately want? What was his game?

Whenever someone took to the skies from here to Cabo San Lucas, they risked getting dive-bombed. And now he wanted my shop. Things started to make sense. No doubt he wanted to take over the whole industry and lifestyle of hang gliding.

Every industry must face this sort of rogue monster sooner or later, I thought to myself, not knowing a single thing about any other industry, really. Once you figure out the answer to a mystery in your own small world, it's easy to extrapolate so that it applies to other parts of the universe. This is how a healthy mind learns, grows, and copes with that which can never truly be understood. Thanks to the powerhouse brainfood of Gorilla BBQ, I felt pretty confident about a whole slew of original conclusions.

Next, I went by my shop. Jethro and his gang were all there. The door was wrenched off its hinges and the sound of evil merriment could be heard from as far away as the Dominoes, about two blocks down the street.

I entered.

"I want everyone out of here," I said.

They laughed, Jethro the loudest.

"Make us," they taunted.

"I'll call the cops!"

"Yeah? But you won't. That's a violation of the code of hang gliders."

Jethro was right. Hang gliders aren't supposed to call upon earthly authorities to resolve hang glider-related disputes. It's a sacred pact we hold with Icarus, god of getting too close to the sun. Rather than doing the prudent thing and backing away, he kept on going until his wings got scorched. This story has been given a few obvious interpretations. To hang gliders, it primarily means that you don't call the cops in matters of hang glider diplomacy.

I stepped right up to Jethro's ugly, aerodynamic face.

"All I know is, one, this is my shop, two, you should leave Jessica out of this, since she doesn't even like hang gliding, and three, I could dive bomb the wings off you any day of the week, with my eyes closed, in the fog."

I got myself pretty beat up after that. So much for standing up for oneself. I spent that night in emergency care.

In the morning, Jessica came to visit me in the hospital.

"I still think hang gliding is scary and pretty lame," she said. "Why don't you just leave flying to birds and American Airlines—and take up landscape painting or something?"

"But I worked my whole life for that shop," I cried, sobbing through my eye bandages.

Jess patted my shoulder. "I'm sorry, Sam" she said. "I remember, one time, I used to be super religious. So, I know how it is to get really attached to believing in the intrinsic goodness of something."

"What about now?"

"I love to sing."

"Can you sing to me?"

"Sure, but not here. It's too quiet here. Somebody might complain."

"That's true."

Jess started attending Skyline College. She hopes to eventually transfer to a school where the cost of living is as cheap as possible. I don't blame her. The Bay Area is overpriced as hell.

Jethro never got hold of my shop. Legal ownership of property is something he could never figure out, even when prepared to bend the rules and regulations.

Some rumors say Jethro's henchmen got sick of dangerous aerial exploits without proper compensation and eventually beat him up and took away all his hang gliders, which they sold to a pawnshop on Mission Street. Others say his crew simply got bored with hang gliders and went back to their Harleys.

Either way, I continue to spend my evenings perched atop of the Korean Baptist Church, waiting for Jethro to appear out of the fogbank. Where there is a fogbank and a strong ocean breeze, rest assured, there will one day be a Jethro, and others like him.

The friendly Korean churchgoers look upon me as their protector. Even though none of them have ever been big into hang gliding, a number of them are adamant ocean fishers, which puts them under my general sphere of that which I have no interest in seeing Jethro bring to harm.

"How goes the coastal patrol this evening?"

I looked down. It was the head pastor of the Korean Baptist Church.

"Pretty good!" I called.

He bowed and I gave a thumbs up. When the church service started, I flew off to practice my dive bombs.

END

Made in the USA
Las Vegas, NV
08 February 2024